Carter

Carter

BOURBON & BLOOD
Book Three

CHASITY BOWLIN

Carter
Paperback Edition
Copyright © 2025 by Chasity Bowlin

Love N. Books Press
An Imprint of Wolfpack Publishing
1707 E. Diana Street
Tampa, FL 33610

www.lovenbookspress.com

Cover design by Jennilynn Wyer Designs
Edited by My Brother's Editor

Carter was originally self-published in 2024 by Chasity Bowlin.

Paperback ISBN 979-8-89567-132-0
Ebook ISBN 979-8-89567-131-3
LCCN 2025942260

Dedication

This isn't a dedication so much as an acknowledgment. I have so many wonderful and amazing people who have supported me, cheered me on, bought my books, reviewed my books, and just kept me going when working a full-time day job, trying to have a life and a house and what amounted to a more than a full-time writing career...all at the same time. For five years, I've been doing this. Now, I'm transitioning to part time at the day job, slowly phasing it out through the remainder of the year. And it's because of all of you wonderful people that I am able to truly live my dream of being "just" an author. Thank you for the love, the support, and the continued friendship.

Carter

One

"What the hell are you doing?"

The woman, a petite and curvy thing with a mile and a half of long, dark hair, glowered down at him from her perch on the bar.

"I don't answer to you, Carter Hayes!" The response was punctuated by the toss of first one, and then another, incredibly high-heeled shoe. Each one hit him square in the chest before tumbling to the floor.

"Josie—" What could he say? She didn't answer to him. They were acquaintances at best.

A few years apart in school, they barely knew one another. But what he did know of her was inconsistent with what was currently on display. Josie Marcum did not dance on bars in seedy dives. In fact, she didn't go to seedy dives, and she sure as hell didn't do it in a slip of a dress that hugged every curve and mile-high heels.

She climbed to her feet, swaying to the music with a seductive rhythm. The men in the bar cheered as she moved her hips side to side. The lush curve of her bottom

1

drew every eye. He noted the slimeball she'd walked in with was watching the show appreciatively.

Carter was no angel. He'd never claimed to be and honestly had no desire for the title. Sinning was too much fun. But he'd never stand by while a woman he'd brought to a bar literally showed her ass in front of other men.

A pirouette went a little sideways, and she wobbled on her feet for a second before tumbling backward. Carter calmly stepped forward and caught her.

"I'm taking you home," he said simply.

"I don't want to go home! I want to dance...and I want another one of those drinks!" she insisted. "Oh, it was yummy."

"How many of those drinks have you had?" he demanded as he set her on her feet just long enough to reclaim her shoes.

"Just the one...but it was so good. And now everything is *spinny*. And shiny. All the lights!" Each word became progressively more slurred.

Carter turned back to her just as she swayed on her feet. She didn't fall so much as she simply deflated, just like someone let the air out of a balloon. Catching her before she fell to the floor, Carter swung her up in his arms again with a curse and headed for the door. He could hear shouts and catcalls from behind him. How any man could get excited by the idea of a half-conscious—or less —woman was a mystery to him.

"Saturday night," he muttered, heading for his truck. "All I wanted was a beer. Now I'm babysitting a pint-sized girl who can't hold her liquor."

Depositing her in the passenger seat, he leaned over to fasten her seat belt. It wasn't that he wanted to be a perv, but the straps of her dress had slipped down just enough that he couldn't not look. The lace of her bra was barely visible, and he felt like an asshole for even thinking that it would have been nice if the straps had slipped a little more.

Seat belt fastened, Carter rose just as someone came barreling out of the bar toward them. It was the dude who'd brought Josie to the shithole bar—a slimly little fucker in sparkly jeans that belonged on a girl. He had a popped collar and every other hallmark of a douchebag.

"Hey, where the hell are you taking her?" Out of the bar, away from the friends or drunk acquaintances who'd been egging him on, the guy's voice was more apologetic than authoritative.

"I'm taking her home...where she can sober up! What the hell was she drinking in there?" he demanded. "More to the point, what the hell did you put in that drink? She might be the size of a ten-year-old, but one drink shouldn't do that!"

"It was just a little something to loosen her up. She said she wanted to have fun tonight!"

The asshole's tone was defensive, laying all the blame at Josie's door. It was the oldest trick in the book. God, he wanted to punch the fucker in the face so bad he it was killing him.

"What did you give her?" Carter asked.

"Dude, it was like half an Ambien. I wanted to fuck her...not kill her. You want her purse or not?" he asked, holding out the small bag.

Carter closed the distance and took the ridiculous beaded clutch from the other man. He waited the space of two heartbeats and then drew back his fist, plowing it straight into the guy's nose. Bone crunched, and blood began to gush immediately. Carter smiled.

"You broke my fucking nose!"

Carter shoved the guy to the ground and grabbed his

wallet from his back pocket. Flipping through the credit cards until he found a driver's license, he nodded.

"I ever hear of you drugging another girl, I ever hear of your breathing in Josie's direction again..." He paused and glanced back at the license. "Shawn Mitchum, I will break more than your goddamn nose. You'll be pissing through a tube for the rest of your life, asshole."

Carter stepped back and watched the guy scramble to his feet. Still clutching his broken nose, he hobbled into the bar. Walking back to the truck and the barely conscious Josie, Carter tucked her purse in beside her and muttered, "You have shitty taste in men, cupcake."

The room was spinning. Josie forced her eyes open and immediately wished she hadn't. Her head hurt. Not just hurt, it felt like it was being split in half with a hammer and chisel. It also felt like there were a thousand grains of sand and a few generously sized shards of glass in her eyes.

Rolling onto her side, she realized it wasn't just her head that ached, but her whole body. *Everything* hurt from head to toe. Her stomach rolled, and she cupped her hand over her mouth in panic.

Those weren't her sheets. She didn't own dark-blue sheets that smelled like really good men's cologne. Where the hell was she?

Scrambling to her feet, the sheet fell away, and she realized that she was wearing a man's T-shirt. Her hair was a hot mess in a way it could only be if she'd slept on it wet. What the hell had happened last night?

"Cupcake, you know how to tie one on in epic proportion."

Oh god. She knew that voice. She knew that snarky tone. A glance over her shoulder confirmed it. Carter Hayes, in all of his glorious half-country boy, half-hipster glory, stood there smirking at her like she was a world-class idiot. He looked hot. And she looked homeless.

Wearing an ancient T-shirt that was so faded it was illegible and a pair of jeans that fit him to perfection, his dark hair had been pulled up in the manliest of buns, and his face was covered with just the right amount of scruff. It was the kind of scruff that made you think about what it would feel like on your skin. If humiliation could be fatal, she'd have been pronounced dead the second she recognized his voice.

"Why am I here? Where are my clothes?" she demanded. The shrill note of her own voice had her wincing and grabbing her head where it threatened to simply implode.

"Easy there, sunshine. First, you don't remember a thing because your shitty-ass *date* slipped an Ambien into your drink last night. And for the record, you ever go near that punk-ass bitch again, I will turn you over my knee."

That rankled. She felt like hammered ass, and he was standing there telling her what she could and could not do.

"You are not the boss of me, Carter Hayes!"

"Someone needs to be, Josephine Marcum," he shot back. "Do you have any idea what could have happened to you last night?"

That gentle reprimand settled her down quickly. She sank back onto the edge of the bed. "Why would he do that?"

Carter raised his eyebrows. "I know your dad is a preacher and all, but surely, at some point in your life,

5

someone explained to you that men have penises, and they like to put them—"

"Stop!" She did not need a sex education lecture from the man who'd single-handedly educated half the female population of Fontaine on a decidedly personal level. "I just wanted to go out and have a few drinks and dance!"

"Because he's a world-class idiot," he replied evenly. "Now, he's an idiot with a broken nose." He smiled at her. "You're welcome."

Josie wanted to crawl back under the covers and never get out. Except, of course, they were his covers, and they smelled like him and even, in her current state of utter misery, that still smelled really, really good.

"Where are my clothes?" She forced herself to ask. She remembered portions of the night, but others were just a huge blank.

"Your dress...well, I had to wash it. You got sick, and it wasn't pretty," he explained, and sounded equal parts amused and sympathetic.

She'd puked her guts out in front of the hottest man in Fontaine. Josie dropped her head to her knees and willed herself not to cry from the humiliation.

"You're not the first person to throw up in my truck," he offered conversationally. "Hell, I've lost count at this point. At least you're not a crier."

Pushing her still damp and crazy hair out of her face, she asked, "Why is my hair still wet?"

He ducked his head, but that did nothing to hide the grin that quirked his perfectly sculpted lips. "Honey, you didn't just puke on your dress. I was half tempted to call a priest."

"I cannot be here," she said. "I cannot be here, and this cannot be happening."

"I'll take you home when you're ready," he offered.

And have everyone in Fontaine talking about it. No. Absolutely not. That could not happen.

"Can you take me to Cincinnati? I need to get my car?"

He frowned at her. "You shouldn't drive yet. If it was just alcohol, you'd be fine, but whatever that dumbass slipped you...you should be careful for a while."

So have everyone in town gossip about her, or risk going to jail for DUI. The options just kept getting better. If her parents knew, *if her father's congregation knew,* she'd never hear the end of it.

Deciding to be honest, she said, "Carter, I can't have anyone see you taking me home."

"You're a big girl, cupcake...well, you're an adult anyway," he corrected with a smirk.

Short jokes were not the best way to endear anyone to her. "It's like this, Carter...I could have spent the night with anyone in this town, and it would be a scandal. But spending it with you, when you're known for being the biggest manwhore to ever live and breathe, is especially bad. My father would never forgive me, and my mother would either die of the shame or make me wish I had."

That stung more than a little. Carter knew his reputation. Hell, he'd made a point to cultivate it in just that way. His mother had always warned him about breaking hearts, and he'd figured out early on that girls didn't get their hearts broken if they didn't expect the heart to ever be involved. But to have this little girl, and he wasn't just talking about her height, tell him that he wasn't good enough to be seen with, that cut deep. It didn't matter

7

that she'd said nothing that wasn't true. He knew just how vicious Fontaine's gossip mill could be.

Shoving his hands into the pockets of his jeans, he rocked back on his heels. "I get it, cupcake. I'm good enough to save your ass, but not good enough to be seen with. There are extra sweatpants in the top drawer. Get dressed, and I'll drive you to get your car."

Carter turned away and headed into the living room. His apartment was the upper floor of Revision, his cousin's salvage and antique store. He worked for Savannah, delivering furniture and hauling shit that she couldn't carry, and did some woodworking on the side with Bennett. The rest of the time, he did construction and odd jobs, none of which helped to alleviate his image as a ne'er-do-well.

Still, looking around the place he'd made for himself, he was proud of it. The heart pine floors he'd refinished himself. The exposed brick he'd chiseled free of layers of plaster, paint, and wallpaper. The furniture was an eclectic mix of old, new, and handmade. The apartment had been his way of saying that he wasn't what other people thought of him, even if few people ever set foot in it. He wasn't afraid of hard work. He just didn't like doing it on other people's terms.

The bedroom door opened, and Josie emerged, drowning in a pair of his sweatpants and his shirt. It shouldn't have looked good on her, and a part of him deeply resented the fact that it did. She'd insulted him, she'd looked down her nose at him, and yet, staring at her in clothes that hung off her like shapeless sacks, he still remembered how she'd looked in that tiny slip of a dress. There was something about her.

"I don't have any shoes," she said.

"You had them last night," he shot back. "You've got

pretty good aim with them too. Besides, I don't think those mile-high heels would be the best fashion choice with your current ensemble."

She glanced down at the baggy T-shirt and sweats, tugging the pants up and folding the waistband over again, and then another time for good measure. They still dragged the floor.

"Probably not," she agreed. "But I really loved those shoes. They made me feel tall."

"Not to put too fine a point on it, but I think that was probably the bar you were dancing on," he offered as he grabbed his keys off the table by the door. "You didn't keep your shoes on long enough for them to do that."

Opening the door, Carter took one look at the steps and then looked back at her. The iron steps were treacherous under the best of circumstances. With the rain from the night before, her bare feet, and pants that were long enough to trip both of them, he just scooped her up in his arms.

She smacked his chest. "Put me down!"

"No," he said, and kept walking.

"I can walk, Carter. This is ridiculous. I'm a grown woman. I don't need to be carried just so you can feel like a he-man!"

"I feel like a he-man, regardless." He couldn't stop the grin that spread across his face. She was so tiny and yet so prickly—like a rabid little hedgehog. "I'm carrying you because if my driving you home would be the height of humiliation for you, winding up with a concussion at the bottom of my steps would probably be even worse. Especially since I happen to know you're not wearing any panties under that getup."

She blushed, her cheeks turning bright pink. "Speaking of which...where are my panties? I found the dress hanging in the bathroom, but the panties are nowhere to be seen."

"You really did throw up a lot. It went everywhere," he said. "As for the panties...I need a souvenir, don't I?"

"Forget it. Just get me back to my car so I can put this whole mess behind me," she said through clenched teeth. Her jaw was so tight it was a wonder the muscles didn't simply snap.

Reaching the bottom of the steps, he didn't put her down, but continued to carry her until he reached his truck. Opening the door, he deposited her on the ancient and cracked vinyl seat in a repeat of the previous night's actions. He walked around to the driver's side and was climbing behind the wheel just as she reached behind her and dug out one high-heeled shoe that was protruding from the seat.

"I don't guess the other one is in here, is it?" she asked.

"It might be. I'll poke around later and see if I can't find it," he offered. "Of course, I can't exactly bring it to you now, can I?"

It still stung. Hell, he knew his reputation. It had never bothered him before. Why it was pissing him off now was a mystery.

He glanced at her out of the corner of his eye. Yes, he did know. He wanted her. Somehow, without him realizing it, Josephine Marcum had become one of the sexiest women he'd ever met. Beautiful, smart, feisty as hell, and all bundled up in a petite, curvy body...yeah, he was sunk.

"If you find my shoe, just bring it to the library. Discreetly, of course," she said primly.

He couldn't stop the grin that spread across his face at her tone. She'd be a wildcat if she ever let loose, he thought. "I like that."

"What?"

He was poking the bear, or the wildcat, in this case. "Your librarian voice, all prim and proper. You're sitting there in my pants, not a stitch on under them, and still on a moral high horse tall enough to kill you if you fall."

The glare he received in response to that made it completely worthwhile.

"I really don't like you."

Carter smiled wider. "Then maybe you should give me back my pants."

As they pulled onto the road, she made not a sound. But if looks could kill, Josie Marcum would have laid him out in two seconds flat.

They'd reached the end of Main Street, where it connected to the highway that would take them back to the scene of the crime, when Josie began to flail about in the seat. Carter turned toward her just as she managed to unbuckle the seat belt and slide all the way down to the floor. She was tucked under the dash like a stowaway.

"What the hell are you doing?" he demanded.

"My parents!" she hissed back at him in a low whisper. "They're coming this way!"

Carter looked up and saw them across the intersection. They were facing them, but with the sun so low in the sky, he doubted they would have seen her.

"You don't have to whisper. The truck's engine is loud enough that they couldn't hear you if even if you yelled...which you do seem to do an awful lot."

"Carter, I can't let them see me like this!"

The desperation was real. She wasn't being melodramatic or carrying on for effect. And it wasn't embarrassment either. This was something else altogether.

"Why, Josie? Just tell me why."

She looked up at him, and the hurt he saw in her eyes was almost too much to bear.

"Because I can't disappoint them. Ever. They saved me, and everyone in this town knows it. If I don't live up to that, Carter, I'll never live it down."

"What the hell does that mean?" he demanded, coasting through the light after it changed.

William Marcum gave him a wave, but there was little warmth in his smile. Of course Carter knew he hadn't done a whole lot to endear himself to the local ministerial association. The bastard son of a drunken criminal and a girl who should have known better, everyone in town had expectations of him, but none of them were good.

"It means that everyone in this town looks up to them. They always tell Mommy and Daddy how good it was of them to bring me home, what wonderful people they are to have adopted a child from such a horrible place. If I embarrass them—"

Frustrated, he slapped his palm against the steering wheel. "Fucking hell, Josie! They're not going to send you back!"

"No," she agreed. "They won't. But I don't ever want them to wish they had."

He hated Fontaine in that moment. Josie's being adopted was no secret. And over the years, he'd heard the talk often enough. Everyone always told her how lucky she was, how grateful she ought to be. But what that really boiled down to was people saying she'd gotten lucky and had been given something she hadn't earned or didn't deserve. Ultimately, they were saying the same thing to her that they always said to him. *You're not good enough.*

"Your parents love you, and you don't put conditions on that," he said softly, reaching down to help her up off the floor.

"It feels like there are conditions," she admitted. "Make good grades. So I did. Make better grades. So I did.

Don't date that boy because he's trouble, so I didn't. I've never once gone against the things they've told me to do... until last night. And you see what a disaster that turned out to be."

"It doesn't look so bad from here," he answered. "You're more than where you come from, Josie Marcum."

And so was he, even if no one would ever believe it.

Two

Josie rolled onto her side as the phone buzzed on the nightstand. She smiled as she saw the name on the screen. In the week since he'd rescued her, nightly phone calls and daily texts had become a thing.

"You have the wrong number," she said as she answered.

"How can you be sure?" he replied suggestively. "You don't even know what I want yet."

But God above, she wanted to. "Behave, Carter."

He chuckled. "Where's the fun in that, cupcake? But since you won't misbehave with me, I guess I'll have to."

He didn't mean it. She knew that. Carter flirted the way most men breathed. It just happened whether he intended to or not. Deciding to move the conversation to safer waters, she asked, "What wonderful things did you find at that auction in Florence today?"

He sighed. "The house had been picked pretty clean by the time we got there. Got a few windows that Savannah will probably have me turn into something crazy.

We did manage to get a real pretty mantle, but I think that's just because the damn thing was marble, and no one else wanted to carry it. Thank God we made Emmitt go."

She giggled at the idea of Emmitt attending an auction surrounded by antique dealers. Carter's mountain of a cousin terrified most people, but he'd always been kind to her. He'd taken excellent care of every stray she'd ever carried up to his door, and there'd been more than a few over the years.

"So you have to give me all the details," she urged.

"About the mantle?" he asked. "It was heavy as shit. What other details do you need?"

If he'd been in front of her, she would have smacked him for being obtuse.

"About Bennett and Mia Darcy," she said. Rumors had been swirling all over town about the two of them, their secret engagement, and the family feud between the Darcy and Hayes clans. It was the stuff of romantic dreams. And now the daring rescue, with Bennett pulling Mia to safety after she crashed her car in a flooded creek. It was definitely swoon-worthy.

"Jesus," he muttered. "Bennett pulled her out of the water. That's all I know. That's all I want to know."

"You don't think it's romantic?" she asked. "He saved her. After all those years of pining for her, he risked his life—"

"Bennett is a Boy Scout, Josie. It could have been Samuel Darcy in that damn creek, and he would have pulled the son of a bitch out. That's just who Bennett is. Don't be reading more into this than there is. It's not a romance novel. It's not one of those damn Lifetime movies you love."

"You don't have an ounce of romance in your soul, do

you?" Josie demanded. "You can't tell me that Bennett doesn't still have feelings for her."

"I'm sure he does." Carter agreed. "But it's not my fault he's a dumbass."

"Carter, I've seen them...out in public, when they run into each other. It's like the air is just charged around them. You have to see that they belong together?"

He sighed again, this time sounding more than a little irritated. "What I see is that she broke his heart once. She walked out on him without a backward glance, and given half the chance, she'll do it again. I'm not going to be Team Mia, Josie. Ever."

He was unreasonable. "And people think Emmitt is the sourpuss! Clearly, they've never heard you on this subject!"

The last thing Carter wanted to talk about was Mia Darcy. He'd gotten used to his nightly phone calls with Josie, of talking to her while he pictured her lying in bed wearing something white, innocent, and still sexy as fuck. It bugged the hell out of him that Mia Darcy was now fucking that up too. She was in Bennett's head, making him crazy. The whole family was in an uproar over it, but no one said anything to Bennett. No. They came to him and had *him* talk to Bennett. Or distract Bennett. Or try to talk some sense into Bennett. He was done with it all.

"Dammit, Josie. Can we not just talk about something else?" he asked.

"Fine," she said, and from the clipped tone of her voice, he knew she was pissed. Lord, she could go from rainbows and kittens to daggers and bullets in two seconds flat.

Since there was no hope in hell of putting that cat back in the bag, he decided just to poke it and see what happened. "You could tell me what you're wearing."

"Ooooooh!"

And there it was. He'd rendered her speechless, left her hissing, spitting, clawing, and probably throwing shit. His work was done.

"Listen here, Carter. I'm not one of your floozies. I'm not chasing after you. I'm not sleeping with you. I'm not having phone sex with you."

"I didn't ask you to," he pointed out reasonably. "I just asked you what you're wearing. It's supposed to get cold tonight, Josie, and you're so little that it wouldn't take much to turn you into a popsicle."

She was probably going to key his truck. No. No one would bother, he reminded himself. Hell, they'd have to find a spot that was more paint than rust.

The sound of her taking deep breaths and counting slowly made him grin. "I don't know what makes you fly off the handle like that, darlin'. I really don't."

"I ought to change my number," she said. "I swear, you just enjoy pissing me off."

He didn't even bother to deny it. "You do look awfully cute when you're mad. Want to snap a pic and send it to me?"

"No. I don't. And I'm wearing something hideous," she said. "Thermal, even. Something so unsexy it'll mark me for life."

He didn't laugh at that. "Josie, haven't you figured out by now that it's not what you're wearing? It's just the fact that it's you."

She sighed then. He could hear her flopping back on

the bed, the springs of the ancient iron bed bouncing. Lord, did that give him filthy ideas. She'd sent him one picture of her lying on that bed, fully clothed, nothing even remotely suggestive about it, but it had fueled more fantasies than the Playboy magazines he'd stolen from Emmitt as a kid.

"What are we doing, Carter? I think we're friends, and then you say things like that. I just don't know what to do."

"We are friends," he replied, kicking off his boots and lying back on his own bed. He stared up at the ceiling and wished with everything in him that she was there with him. "But we're not just friends, Josie. Or at least that's not what I want us to be."

"Carter—"

"Don't say no," he urged. "Just think about it. If you decide it's not worth the risk, fine...I'll never bring it up again. But you wanted fun, Josie. Your words, not mine."

"I know that," she answered.

"I can make it fun, Josie." He'd use every damn thing he'd learned. It wouldn't be just fun. It'd be unforgettable. Carter knew that if he could get her in his bed once, he could keep her there, at least long enough to get her out of his system.

"*If*..." She began. "I agreed, it would have to be a secret. I won't be just another name on the list."

"There is no list," he replied. Half the women he was rumored to have slept with were nothing more than friends, and the other half, well, he hadn't broken any promises to anybody. "And I don't give a damn what anyone thinks but you. I can be as discreet as you need me to be."

"I have to think. I'll let you know," she said.

Which meant he'd overplayed his hand and would likely never hear from her again. Fuck.

Three

Carter answered his phone, knowing it wouldn't be a call from the one person he wanted to hear from. Since their conversation the day after Mia's accident, he hadn't heard a word from her. And now, Bennett was losing his shit, which was undoubtedly the reason his mother was calling.

"Hey, Mama," he said. He could see his plan of going to the bar and getting completely shitfaced, and maybe bringing home some Amazon woman who'd make him completely forget about his own little pixie from hell, going down the toilet.

Lynnette Hayes clucked her tongue at him like a worried hen. "Carter, you need to go pick up Bennett and head out to Emmitt's. That boy needs to clear his head. Some good, hard work on the farm will fix him right up."

It wouldn't. The only thing that would fix Bennett up was climbing right back into Mia Darcy's pants, but that caused a whole slew of new problems, and he sure as hell wasn't about to say that to his mother. Lord, he wanted to be done with it all. He wanted to not be assigned to take care of poor, brokenhearted Bennett or to lure surly ass Emmitt out of his house or keep Savannah from letting her mouth write checks her ass couldn't cash. For someone that was a reputed layabout, he sure as hell didn't get a moment's peace from people asking him to fix things.

"Yes, ma'am. I'm on my way to Bennett's now. Emmitt already texted me."

Lynnette grew quiet. "Emmitt can text? Does he say more that way than he does in person?"

Carter laughed out loud in spite of his shitty mood. He couldn't help it. "No. Not really. And yes, in spite of the fact that his hands are the size of a Christmas ham, he can text."

"All right, then. Get Bennett out there and let him work off some of the mad...or whatever else it is that's got him wound up like a long-tailed cat. And don't drink too much while you're out there! You boys act like fools when you get drunk!"

Carter pulled his truck into Bennett's driveway, knowing his mother was watching from her front window across the street. Climbing out of the truck, he waved a little and headed for the porch. From the corner of his eye, he saw a streak of movement across the backyard. Turning his head fully, he caught sight of Mia Darcy's retreating form as she sped through the woods and back to her very own ivory tower.

"Shit," he muttered, as he opened the door to let himself in. Bennett was standing in the kitchen looking poleaxed, for lack of a better word. "Dude, what the fuck?"

"Mind your own business, Carter," Bennett snapped, but he didn't bother to turn around.

That pissed him off. Hell, when Bennett had mooned

over her a decade ago, Carter had been the one to drag him kicking and screaming back to the land of the living.

"Last time I checked, you were still my blood...and she's still the woman who tried to rip your heart right out of your chest, just like in the Temple of Doom, so I figure that makes it my business." There was no way this was going to go well. Bennet would be heartbroken. The whole town would be talking about them. *Again.* And any time a Hayes tangled with a Darcy, Samuel would start calling favors. Property taxes doubled, mortgages were suddenly called in, or payments were misplaced. That man had fucked them over more times than any of them could count.

"You figured wrong. I can handle this." Bennet had poured them both glasses of bourbon as he spoke.

Carter laughed—hard. He bent over double with his hands on his knees and laughed until he couldn't breathe. The sheer ridiculousness of Bennett, the original love-sick fool, telling him he could handle it was just too much. Finally, breathless and wiping tears from his eyes, Carter rose to his full height and shook his head.

"You're so damn dumb I almost feel sorry for you."

Bennett passed him a glass of bourbon and a warning look to accompany it. "I get that you don't have more than a passing acquaintance with sympathy, Carter, but in general, people don't express it by laughing so hard they damn near piss themselves."

"Can't help it," Carter replied, taking the glass and slamming the bourbon before handing it back for a refill. It burned like fire, but damn, it was worth it. What he had to say wouldn't be taken well, but that didn't make it any less true. "It's funny now. But when she chews you up and spits you out again, none of us will be laughing. We don't need another reason to hate the Darcys. We got plenty already."

The Darcys had been his family's enemy for so long that he wasn't even sure why they all hated one another. He just knew that it ran deep, and Bennett and Mia would never not be caught in the middle of it. They both needed to accept it and move the hell on.

After a long pause, Bennett nodded. "You've made your point. Why are you here?"

Carter shrugged, trying to make it appear casual and not like the whole family plotted to get him out of the house and away from temptation.

"Emmitt's tearing down that old barn today. Figured a little destruction might improve your mood."

"You're driving," Bennett said as he moved toward the door. "You've had less bourbon."

Carter followed Bennett outside and then climbed behind the steering wheel. Bennett was shifting in the seat, digging between the cushions until his hand emerged, clutching a very tiny and very pointy high-heeled shoe. He cocked an eyebrow at Carter.

"Changing up your wardrobe a little?"

Carter eyed the shoe for a minute and then smiled. That was his in. She wanted that shoe back, and she'd have to see him to get it. He laughed.

"She said she lost that in here. I thought she made it up to have an excuse to come back!" he joked.

"Who?"

Carter shook his head. He was keeping that to himself. Not just because Josie would never want anyone to know, but because he didn't want the humiliation of having it blow up in his face when she more than likely rejected him.

"Like I'm gonna tell!"

"So you can butt your big-ass nose into my business, but I'm not allowed to know yours?" Bennett groused.

Carter took the shoe and tossed it behind the seat. "That's not 'business.' That was one wild, crazy, and fantastic night that will never be repeated. No harm, no foul," he lied. Deciding to turn the tables, he said, "This thing with you and Mia is going to bring hell down on all of us. You know that, right?"

Bennett sighed. "I know."

For the longest time, they sat there in silence until Carter finally turned the key in the ignition. Carter thought about Josie, about the scandal he was courting, about the risks, and about all the things the upright citizens of Fontaine would have to say about both of them.

So he asked Bennett the burning question, "Is she worth it?"

"A million times over," Bennett admitted.

It wasn't Mia Darcy on his mind then. It was Josie Marcum standing in the middle of his bedroom in a T-shirt that covered her to her knees. He was starting to understand where Bennett was coming from.

"Then do what you gotta do, and we'll sort out the mess later."

Carter drove the short distance to the farm and turned onto the rutted gravel road, the truck bumping so furiously that Bennett very nearly came off the seat.

"You gotta get a new truck, man. This thing is a death trap."

It was true, but Carter loved that truck. He held on to it out of nothing but sentiment. They all knew it. He could have bought another one years earlier and chose not to.

Bennett shook his head. "Fine. Keep this junk heap.

And keep your secrets about whatever girl it was who lost a Barbie-sized shoe in here."

Carter shook his head as he eased the truck into a parking space beside Emmitt's monster SUV. "I'm not giving up this truck. It's a classic. Do you know how many hours Papaw and I spent working on this thing together?"

Bennett was still shaking his head as he climbed out. "Not a damn one of us can count that high. From the time you were old enough to hold a wrench, you were covered in grease. Let's go make Emmitt do all the work while we drink all his beer."

That had been Carter's plan all along.

Josie glanced at her phone for the fourteenth time in the last hour. She'd gotten used to daily texts from Carter. Now that they'd stopped, she missed them terribly. She missed *him*.

Carter had always said something that just hovered on the edge of inappropriate. That boy—No, he was not a boy. He was a man. He was definitely all man. And a master of the art of the double entendre. If she even questioned him about anything he'd said, he'd lay the blame squarely at her door and call her a pervert. It was infuriating and frustrating and...fun.

He'd given her the one thing she'd been missing in her life. *Not the only thing*. The unhelpful voice at the back of her mind reminded her of their last conversation and the offer that was still on the table. It'd expire eventually. He wouldn't wait forever for her to decide, and she couldn't for the life of her figure out why she was being such a coward about it.

Because once he has you, he won't want you anymore.

Again, with the unhelpful voice. Well, it was helpful, but way more truthful than she wanted to admit. That very idea terrified her. She didn't want to be just one of Carter's women. She wanted to be different and special, and it terrified her. Because Carter Hayes, while he was a good time, and not just in the phone number on a bathroom wall kind of way, was also special. He was funny and far smarter than anyone, including himself, gave him credit for. And while she'd always thought he was good-looking, she had entered full-blown crush territory and was watching her phone like an idiot teenager.

A glance at the clock confirmed that it was almost time to leave for the day. Her shift at the library ended at five, and since she'd woken up in his bed, not a day had gone by that he hadn't at least said hello to her.

"Well, it's not like we're dating," she said aloud, her voice barely more than a whisper. "He's Carter Hayes. He doesn't do relationships, anyway. It's just harmless flirtation that's not intended to go anywhere."

"Shhhh!"

The admonishment had come from the head librarian, Doris Byers, who was glaring at her from the opposite stack as they re-shelved returned books. Josie ducked her head and returned to the task at hand. She was already on Doris's bad side. The woman hadn't wanted to hire her to begin with, since she'd been eyeing the assistant librarian position for her own niece, who barely knew the alphabet. The city council had intervened, though, and the not-so-subtle hostility that had resulted was damn near impossible to live with.

Josie picked up the last book, and a piece of paper fluttered to the floor. Bending over, she picked it up and immediately smiled. The surprisingly artistic rendering of a single high-heeled shoe was accompanied by the words, *Have you missed me?*

It had to be Carter. Sparing a glance for Doris, who was staring disapprovingly at a couple of teenagers ensconced in one of the reading nooks, Josie pulled out her phone and tapped the text message on the touchscreen.

Josie
Did you find my shoe?

Carter
Come over and find out. You can park out back, and no one will see you.

Josie considered her options. She really wanted that shoe back. She'd been holding on to the other one in the desperate hope that its mate would be found. And seeing Carter, alone, in his apartment, with no prying eyes...That had an appeal all of its own.

The decision to go to that seedy-ass bar in Cincinnati with a guy she honestly didn't even like had come about because she wanted to have fun, because she wanted to do something wild and totally unexpected. What could be more unexpected than Carter Hayes?

Josie
I'll be there at six. You better have my shoe...and my panties.

Carter
I have no idea what you're talking about. You should be more careful where you leave your lacy Victoria's Secret panties.

Josie
I never said they were Victoria's Secret.
Liar.

Carter
It's just an assumption. You look like a
Vickie kind of girl. Sexy, but still totally
respectable. More satin with a hint of
lace than black leather and fishnet.

She didn't want to be respectable, and she sure as hell didn't want him to think about her that way. Carter made her want to be all kinds of things she'd never considered before. Leather and fishnet didn't seem quite as farfetched to her as they might have at one time.

"Are you going to shelve that book or just stare at your phone all afternoon, Josephine?" Doris demanded, her voice sharp and hateful.

With a guilty flush staining her cheeks, Josie dropped her phone back into the pocket of her shapeless khaki pants. Doris had imposed a dress code almost as soon as she'd been hired, and it was intended to strip every employee of sex appeal, confidence, and the will to live. Josie refused to wear them outside of the library, wearing her own clothes to work and changing in the ladies' room before starting her day.

"Sorry, Doris. It was a reminder about an errand I have to run after work."

"After work, Josephine. That's an important distinction," Doris retorted spitefully.

Josie didn't say anything else. There was nothing she could say that wouldn't be wrong, so instead, she just kept her mouth shut.

Placing the book back on the shelf, she wheeled the cart back to its home behind the circulation desk and then used the computer there to log herself out for the day. She needed to change back into her own clothes before she saw Carter. If he ever saw her in the mom pants she was currently not rocking at all, she'd die of shame.

There was a dress hiding out in the back of her closet. An impulse buy at the mall in Lexington that she'd never had the courage to wear. It was now or never, she thought.

Heading home, she took a quick shower and shaved her legs in record time. After applying lotion and perfume, she touched up her makeup and then went to her closet and retrieved the secret weapon. Slipping the dress on over her head, she tugged the zipper at the side, sucking in everything she possibly could until it finally closed.

One look at the mirror and she almost chickened out. It was cut low—impossibly, indecently, terrifyingly low. It hugged her breasts, pushing them up and amplifying them to epic proportions before nipping in at her waist and then flaring over her hips. The skirt was full but impossibly short, revealing more of her thighs than she'd ever done other than when she was at the beach. On her feet, she wore her second favorite pair of heels—black, strappy, and a mile high. If she were lucky, the top of her head would actually reach his shoulder. God, she hated being short.

Before leaving the house, she grabbed her trench coat and slipped it on. The last thing she needed was her nosy neighbors seeing her slipping out of the house looking like the Whore of Babylon. They'd be on the phone to her father, reporting her sinful ways, before he could even ask for an amen.

Driving through town, most people were already home for the day. Luckily, Fontaine practically rolled up the sidewalks after five. Josie pulled her car around behind

Revision. There was a small alley there where Carter kept his truck. It was cut off from the street, and the only way anyone would see her car was if they actually walked behind the building. It was about as private as you could get in Fontaine, where everyone on the street knew when you peed simply because your next-door neighbor saw the bathroom light turn on and then called in a report.

Climbing from the car, she paused at the bottom of his steps and looked up. Carter stood in the doorway, looking straight at her, a smirk curving his lips.

"What are you looking at?" she demanded. Lord, but he got under her skin.

His smirk stretched into a full-blown, devastatingly sexy grin, right down to the crinkly lines at the corners of his eyes. He looked like a pirate—like a hot, sexy, fantasy pirate.

"The fruits of my labor. I knew if I told you how respectable you were, you'd do your damnedest to look the opposite. You are a contrary creature, Josephine Marcum, but at the moment, that is totally working in my favor."

She hated him. She was still going to seduce him, or maybe let him think he was seducing her. That had yet to be determined. But at some point, they were going to be naked together, and she was going to come back to that whole pirate thing in a big way.

Now or never, Josie. Now or never.

Four

Carter watched her walk up the stairs. He wasn't sure what the hell that dress was made of, but he'd remember to say a prayer of thanks, though that would probably finish paving his road to hell. There was lots of jiggling. Why the hell women tried to avoid having things jiggle when to his mind it was the best damn thing about their bodies, he had no idea.

Every step and her perfect breasts threatened to spill out of the top of that piece of lingerie that was masquerading as a dress. By the time she reached the door, he could barely breathe. He sure as hell couldn't talk. So he just stepped back and ushered her inside.

"I'm feeling a little underdressed." He finally managed as he walked into the kitchen and flipped the steaks he'd put on.

"Dinner? Were you expecting someone else?" she asked.

"Just you. I thought since you'd had to come all this way to retrieve your shoe, I could at least feed you," he replied. It was a way to keep her there longer, a way to get her relaxed enough and at ease enough to charm her right out of that dress and whatever delicious things she was wearing under it.

"Carter, do you really want to have dinner with me?"

He looked back at her. It was a confusing question, but she was a confusing woman. He'd learned that about her the hard way. "Why wouldn't I want to have dinner with you?"

She perched on the arm of the couch, one leg draped over the other. How the hell she could be that short and her legs could look that long was a mystery.

"Carter, we both know I'm not here for my shoe, and you didn't invite me here for dinner...And we both know it isn't steak that I'm hungry for. You've got me where you wanted me. Do something about it."

He turned off the burner. If she wanted to be direct, that was fine with him. Closing the distance between them in three long strides, he closed his arms around her and hauled her against him. Her Cupid's bow lips had been driving him crazy for two damn weeks, but he didn't plan on rushing a thing.

"What are you waiting for?" Josie asked.

"Anticipation isn't a bad thing," Carter replied. "If you're doing it right, it's part of the fun."

Carter slid his hands over her back, mostly bared by the sexy cutouts of the dress. Christ almighty. For such a very good girl, she sure as hell had a bad girl's wardrobe.

"What did you come here for, Josie?" he asked.

"You know," she said, her tone low and accusatory.

He did. But he wanted her to say it. He needed that. "You've got to be the one to say it, cupcake."

"I want to be in your bed, Carter...and this time I don't want to be in it alone." Her reply was little more than a whisper as she strained toward him, coming up onto her tiptoes. "I know you're not shy."

He grinned at that, twining his fingers through the cascade of her dark hair. "No, baby, I'm not shy at all. But when it's all said and done, I want us both to know that you didn't just fall from grace...you jumped willingly."

She laughed. "I squeezed my ass into this dress so you could peel me out of it. Think we can get to that sometime tonight?"

Carter lifted her completely and then tossed her back onto the couch. Her skirt hiked up, revealing a tantalizing glimpse of black panties. But he didn't linger too long to enjoy the view. Instead, he kneeled on the couch above her, his knee sliding between her silken thighs and his palms bracketing her head, caging her beneath him.

"I've been picturing you like this since the night I saw you dancing on that bar," he said. "Right before you threw your shoes at me."

The last thing Josie wanted to be reminded of was puking all over his truck and herself. That particular humiliation was dying a slow death.

"Can we not talk about that now? Can we not talk right now, period? Jesus, Carter, just kiss me already!"

He did. Oh lord, but he *did*. His lips settled on hers, firm but undeniably gentle, molding to hers so completely that it was impossible to tell where one ended and the other began. It was a slow kiss, just lips tasting, pressing, nuzzling against hers. But still, it made her burn. Then she felt his tongue sliding between her lips, tangling with her own, and she thought she'd die from it.

No one had ever kissed her that way. It was like every nerve ending in her body had simply lit up at the same time. Only their lips were touching. He was still holding himself above her. But that wasn't what she wanted. She needed to feel the hard press of him against her, to feel the weight of him on her as she locked her legs around him.

She lifted her hands and locked them behind his neck, trying to tug him down. He was as immovable as a mountain.

He pulled back from her then, breaking that perfect kiss. "I'm too heavy for you."

It was the story of her damn life. Just because she was little, just because she was short, everyone underestimated her. Everyone thought she was some delicate little thing that needed to be handled with care. She needed Carter Hayes on her. Hell, she needed him in her.

"No, you're not. I'm short, Carter. Not fragile. Now, would you please just fuck me already?"

The look he gave her was scorching. His eyes raked over her, and his hands followed suit. Then his mouth was on hers again—hotter, hungrier, more demanding. And she gave it back to him, measure for measure. He stood suddenly, taking her with him, and strode to the bedroom.

Josie was still clinging to him, arms around his neck and legs locked on his hips, when he lay the two of them down on the bed, his mouth never leaving hers for even a second.

Somehow, without any guidance from her, he managed to find the zipper of her dress. She couldn't hear the rasp of the zipper sliding free over the pounding of her own heart. A low moan escaped her as his hand slipped beneath the fabric, his perfectly callused fingers grazing her ribs.

Even after she'd said the filthiest thing to him that she'd ever uttered in her life, he still wasn't in a hurry. He was just taking his time, drawing lazy circles on her skin with the pad of his thumb. Not that it didn't feel amazing. It did. It really did. But there were other amazing things they could do, and she wanted to get to them. Preferably before she died of old age.

Then he deepened the kiss, parting her lips and sweeping inside. The sensual glide of his tongue against hers, the not-so-gentle nip of his teeth at her lower lip, only heightened everything she felt already. Heat rushed through her, blood pooling in sensitive places, creating that delicious ache that she knew he'd ease in his own good time.

Somehow, the dress simply vanished. He'd slipped it off her arms until it was bunched around her waist, leaving her clad only in the black strapless bra she'd worn beneath it. Then it was gone entirely, stripped off her and tossed aside, and she lay beneath him wearing the skimpiest lingerie she owned. He was still fully clothed. She could feel the soft, faded denim of his jeans against her thighs, the buttons of his shirt against her. It was too much. She wanted his skin on hers—she needed it.

Reaching for the buttons of his shirt, she began undoing them quickly, but her fingers fumbled.

He pulled back from the kiss for just long enough to rip the shirt off and toss it aside. She had a quick glimpse of well-defined pecs and chiseled abs. Carter wasn't big and bulky. Living in a gym would never be his thing, she knew, but his body had been sculpted by hard work, by lifting and tugging and hauling heavy furniture, by working with his hands. Nothing, to her mind, would ever be sexier than that.

Her hands roamed his chest, tracing the ridges of his

abs as he settled against her. The hard press of his body against hers was so good, so perfect, that she didn't want to risk letting go. Following her instinct, she brought her knees up and locked her legs around his lean hips. Through the layers of fabric that remained, she could feel the hard ridge of his erection against her. Arching her hips, moving against him, she smiled at his answering groan.

"I'm trying," he said, "to make this last. I don't want to rush."

"Make it last next time." She urged him. "Do you have any idea how long it's been since I've had sex, Carter? Years. Literally. Years. And even then, it wasn't bad. It just wasn't good."

He grinned, even as he pressed a kiss to the arch of her collarbone. It was followed by a lick that left her shivering. "Then stop rushing and let me make this good for you."

Josie wanted to reply, but he'd moved lower, tugged the cup of her bra down, and the heat of his mouth had closed over one taut peak. She arched her back, offering herself up to him as he teased her nipple with his lips, flicking with his tongue. The gentle bite that followed made her scream. Somehow, he worked his hands under her and freed the clasp, tossing the garment aside. Her hands slid into his thick hair, tugging at it as he turned his attention to her other breast, licking and sucking with equal fervor.

He hooked one hand behind her knee, forcing her to unlock her ankles. Then he moved lower, trailing hot kisses over her stomach. When he kissed her through the black lace of her panties, she shivered. His fingers slipped beneath the elastic band, tugging them down her thighs and then over the ridiculous high heels she still wore.

"I should take those off," she said.

"No," he replied, his hand skimming over her thigh, her calf, all the way down to encircle her ankle. "You shouldn't. Tell me it doesn't feel sexy to be here in my bed, wearing nothing but a pair of hooker heels."

She couldn't because he was so right. It felt decadent and naughty and all those things that she was afraid to be. There was no chance to respond. Having him kiss her through the black lace had made her tremble, but when his mouth descended on her bare flesh, licking along the seam of her sex with slow, deliberate strokes, the whole world just fell away.

Her head fell back, her hands fisted in the bedclothes beneath her, and her breath came in sharp pants as the sensations simply overwhelmed her. He parted the folds of her sex, his tongue circling the hard nub of her clit.

"Carter!" She arched off the bed, gasping and shuddering. His hands closed over hers, his fingers twining through hers. As he drove her higher, his tongue relentlessly stroking her, his hands were her anchor. It felt like she was falling, like the world was simply dissolving beneath her, and the only thing holding her there were the points of contact between them.

The tension coiled so tightly inside her, every muscle quivering as he took her even higher. Every stroke of his tongue, every soft and gentle nip from his teeth, the hot pull of his mouth on her flesh, drove her on.

She wasn't even aware of the sounds she made, of the soft, keening cries that escaped her. She had no control of her body, of the way she arched beneath him, grinding her hips against him. Need had consumed her completely, and when it was finally sated, when the tension broke inside her and pleasure pulsed through her, she collapsed back against the bed, breathless and stunned.

But Carter didn't give her a chance to recover or even

process the fact that she'd just had the most earth-shattering orgasm of her life. He moved over her, reaching into his pocket for a condom. Placing it on the bed, he unzipped his jeans. Of course, she thought, there was no underwear. Why would Carter Hayes ever bow to such convention?

He rolled the condom on with quick, efficient, and far too practiced movements. But that thought faded as he settled himself between her thighs, nudging inside her one slow, glorious inch at a time. He was larger than she'd expected, certainly larger than anyone she'd been with before. He filled her up completely, making it impossible to think, impossible to do anything but feel. With one hand hooked behind her knee, he hitched her thigh higher on his hip, surging deeper as he kissed her tenderly.

If it were possible to die from pleasure, she would have. The gentle kiss was so at odds with the power of his body moving over her, moving inside her, but those two things together simply robbed her of thought. They robbed her of all reason, and she closed her arms tightly around him, her nails digging into his back as she held on.

His lips left hers, trailing kisses over her cheek, her neck. Then his teeth nipped gently at her earlobe. And he continued to rock inside her, to thrust his hips against her, and surge just a little deeper each time. She couldn't even tell where he ended and she began anymore. It was like he'd been meant to be a part of her always.

Her thighs trembled, and her belly quivered as the tension built in her again. Every part of her body was on fire. His hand moved between them, his fingers sliding over her damp flesh, zeroing in on her clit and stroking her with the perfect amount of pressure. Her eyes closed, her lips parted, but she couldn't make a sound. She couldn't even draw breath. Everything in her body had coiled tight, waiting for the implosion.

"Come for me, Josie," he urged her. "You're so close, baby. I can feel it."

His fingers stroked over her again as he pressed into her, and Josie trembled. Her body clenched and then released as wave after wave washed through her. She felt Carter tense against her, heard the harsh groan that escaped him, and knew that he was right there with her.

In a moment of clarity, she realized the horrible mistake she'd made. No one else would ever make her feel the way he just had, and Carter, when it came to women, had a very short attention span.

Shit.

Five

Josie was back at work the following day, trying to pretend her thighs weren't killing her and that she hadn't had her world rocked in more ways than one.

She hadn't spent the night with Carter. He hadn't asked her to. Of course, he hadn't tried to rush her out the door, but she hadn't wanted to risk that happening. Her pride couldn't survive a hit like that. So around midnight, she'd gotten up, gathered her panties, and headed for the door. He'd walked her out, kissed her good night, and handed her back the damn shoe that had started it all.

Glancing at the numbers on the spine of the book, she grimaced. It would be on the bottom shelf. Squatting down, trying not to whimper and trying not to remember the crazy acrobatics from round two that had turned her thighs to Jell-O, Josie put the book back where it belonged. Before she could get back up, a long shadow fell over her. Doris, she thought, and grimaced. But as she glanced up, she realized she couldn't have been more wrong.

Carter stood there, grinning cheekily and looking totally at ease. Not awkward or embarrassed or even slightly ruffled at seeing her. The bastard.

"I need some help finding a book," he said, just loud enough for Doris, who was straining every muscle in her body leaning closer, to hear.

"What is it that you're looking for?"

"The Kama Sutra," he replied softly, without missing a beat. "I looked it up, and you are supposed to have it, but I can't find it on the shelf."

She was going to murder him. "We most certainly do not have that book," she answered. Not that they shouldn't have. If it were up to her, there'd be a lot of books available in the library that Doris frowned upon.

He grinned. "Do you have anything along those lines? I'm really looking to expand my knowledge."

Josie could feel the blush creeping up her cheeks. He did not need to expand his knowledge of anything. And if Doris leaned any further over that counter, trying to hear every word that he said, she was going to wind up flat on her face.

"We have a selection of books that might be to your liking. They're on the second floor. Section H."

"Which way is that? Can you show me? You may not realize this, but I don't spend a whole lot of my time in libraries," he replied. The grin hadn't left his face the whole time. He knew exactly what he was doing. Every female in the building had drifted closer, like he had some kind of weird gravitational pull that attracted estrogen.

Josie sighed. "Come with me," she said, trying to keep her voice as professional as possible.

"I did," he whispered. The grin was gone, and the teasing light in his eyes just vanished. It was all heat and

41

sex, and suddenly she just wanted to be back in his bed with her legs wrapped around him again.

Her knees wobbled as she rose to her full height, which still meant she could walk right beneath his raised arm. She had to squeeze past him to exit the stacks, her breasts brushing against his chest, and his eyes on her the whole time. Her nipples hardened beneath her blouse, and she thanked heaven for padded bras. He knew exactly what that casual touch had done to her, but at least no one else did.

As she crossed the room, she could feel him behind her, walking just close enough to keep up, to occasionally brush against her, but not close enough for any casual observer to think anything of it. She could also feel his eyes on her as she climbed the stairs in front of him. More particularly, she could feel his gaze locked squarely on her ass.

When they reached the second floor, she led him down the hall, and when they were out of sight of prying eyes, grabbed his arm and tugged him between the stacks.

"What the hell are you doing?" She hissed.

"I wanted to see you," he replied, completely unapologetic and unfazed by her temper. "Those few hours last night were not nearly enough."

"Carter, you know I can't be seen with you!"

He moved closer, his big body blocking her in, his arms caging her there. "Why not?"

He knew why. Everyone in town knew why. Because she was the one preacher's kid who hadn't lived up to the wild child stereotype. Yet. Because her father was the pastor of the First Baptist Church of Fontaine, and everyone in town looked up to him. And because if she did anything to make him look bad, he wouldn't be angry, he wouldn't disown her, he'd just give her that cold, steely stare and tell her how horribly disappointed he was in her. Everything wrong she'd ever done in her life had been met with those words, and they just made her want to curl up and die.

"Because we both know that everyone in this town knows what you do. Women are like Kleenex for you, Carter. And with who my parents are, I have a higher standard to live up to than most people!"

His hands closed on her waist, tugging her to him, close enough that she could feel the hardness of him against her. All the reasons she should be pissed, all the reasons that she should push him away and try to keep her distance, just faded from her mind. All she could think about was how it had felt to be consumed by him.

"Carter, I can't." She managed. "Not here. Someone will see."

"Dammit, Josie. I'm not that bad," he snapped. "They're not going to make you wear a scarlet letter!"

First, he was referencing Hester Prynne when Carter reportedly never picked up a book in his life. Second, he was that bad, and they both knew it.

"Yes, you are. Melissa Pelfrey. Natalie Simmons. Carly Masters...and they're just this year!"

"Just because I go out with a woman doesn't mean I sleep with her," he protested.

"Did you sleep with them?" she demanded.

He didn't answer, just stepped back from her, shoved his hands in his pocket, and stared straight ahead. She wished she hadn't asked the question, but it was too late.

"I'm not going to be added to that list of women who chased you around this town like a fool. I'm perfectly willing to keep seeing you, Carter. I want to. But not at the expense of my reputation."

Carter stared at her for a minute, unable to really process what he was hearing. "This isn't Victorian England, Josie!"

"It's Fontaine, Kentucky, Carter Hayes, which amounts to the same damn thing," she replied sharply. "If you don't want to continue this—"

"That's not what I said," he interrupted. The thought of not seeing her again, of not tasting her or touching her, or having her tiny, curvy body straining beneath him... Yeah, that wasn't an option. Somehow or other, the little firecracker had gotten under his skin, and until he figured out how to get her out of his head, he'd just have to play by her rules. Even if they did rankle.

He took a deep breath, tried to calm the tides of both churning anger and stupidity-inducing lust. It stung his pride and, if he were honest, it hurt his feelings a little to be told he was essentially too much of a whore to be seen with. How the hell did that happen?

"Fine, you want to keep this a secret? We'll keep it a secret. We'll sneak around like everyone else in this damn town does."

Josie nodded, clearly satisfied that she had his balls tucked neatly in her handbag. "Then get out of here. I need to finish work, and Doris is all over me."

Carter shuddered. "Please don't phrase it like that. The idea of Doris all over anyone is enough to shrivel my dick for life."

Josie responded with an eye roll as she thrust a book at him. "Go check that out. If you don't leave here with a book, heaven only knows what people will say."

"I don't have a library card," he protested. "I just came

44

in here to mess with your head...and to see if you'd come over tonight."

"Get one. And yes. I'll be there at seven," she said softly as she moved past him and headed back to work.

Standing there holding a book, Carter looked down at the title. *Hard Enough: Overcoming Erectile Dysfunction.* He was still laughing as he carried it to the counter and dutifully checked the book out, just as he'd been told to.

Doris gave him the side eye, staring at the book and then at him.

"It's for Emmitt," he offered. "People always wonder why he's so hateful. Nothing stays a secret forever in this town."

Doris clucked her tongue. "That poor boy."

Carter bit his cheek to keep from laughing. "We're all praying for him, Doris. Every last one of us." Emmitt would kick his ass, but it would probably be worth it. Oh, hell no. It would *definitely* be worth it.

It was just after six when Josie pulled into her driveway. She was scrambling, running late, and in a foul mood. Doris had cornered her before she left for the day, informing her that she felt Josie's job performance was subpar. They both knew that Doris's real complaint was that she and Josie did not share DNA. For years, every single person working in that library had a family connection to her. She resented the city council taking over hiring in what she viewed as her own private domain.

Walking up to the front porch, Josie heard the television inside and frowned. No car in the driveway meant that her father had dropped her mother off for a visit. Great. Just great. That was the last thing she needed.

Forcing a smile, she let herself into the house that her grandmother had all but given to her. Yes, she paid rent, but it was a pittance. Meanwhile, her grandmother was living it up in a retirement community in Florida with a new boyfriend every week.

"Hi, Mom. I wasn't expecting you," she said.

Deborah Marcum smiled. "Does that mean you have plans? Maybe a hot date?"

Yeah. She was never having that conversation with her mother. *I'm going to put on the sluttiest thing I own and let Carter Hayes bend me over his couch.* Yeah. Never. Going. To. Happen.

"No," Josie lied. "Just means I wasn't expecting you. Where's Daddy?"

Deborah settled back in her chair. "He's gone to the hospital to visit a couple that just lost their baby. I just didn't have the heart for it today."

It was undoubtedly an anniversary of one of the many miscarriages her mother had suffered over the years. Out of desperation, they'd adopted Josie from a Ukrainian orphanage when she was barely a year old. That hadn't stopped them from trying desperately over the years for a biological child. And Deborah still grieved for every one that she'd lost.

"I'm sorry. I know those are difficult for you," Josie finally said. "Have you eaten dinner?"

Deborah shook her head. "No. But I'll wait. I have something in the Crock-Pot at home for your father. It'll be better if I eat with him later. He's very worried about you, Josie. You missed church last week, and you missed choir practice last night. We could have used you there.

You know Mildred plays the piano like she has hammers for hands."

"Mom, I told you and Daddy that I couldn't continue playing piano for the choir," Josie began. "With work and taking care of the house, I just don't have time."

"Do you have time to go to bars in Cincinnati?" Deborah asked pointedly.

So that's what it was all about. Dropping her bag onto the floor, Josie settled into one of the other chairs and stared balefully at her mother.

"This is why I moved out. You and Daddy don't get to monitor or control everywhere I go and everything I do."

"Or everyone you're doing it with. Doris informed me that you and Carter Hayes looked very cozy at the library this afternoon."

She hated Fontaine. She fucking hated it, and in that moment, she wasn't overly appreciative of her parents, either. Yes, she loved them. Yes, they'd given her so many opportunities. But she was an adult, and it was her life. She had to be able to make her own decisions.

"Carter came in looking for a book, and I helped him with it. If Doris wants to make more of it than that, it's on her."

Deborah straightened the hem of her skirt, smoothing it with her fingertips. "I'm not unsympathetic, Josie. He's a handsome man...ridiculously so. A boy like that could turn any woman's head. And if you want to have your fun with him, well, there's nothing I can do to stop you. But I'd strongly advise you against letting your heart get involved. That boy is just like his daddy, and he'll never settle down with one woman. Blood tells, Josie."

Josie knew the story. Everyone in town knew the story. Carter's mother and father had never married because, on the eve of their wedding, she'd caught him with her best

47

friend—the woman who'd been her maid of honor. And Carter's father had flitted in and out of his life but never settled, never stuck around when Carter needed him. Eventually, he'd been killed in another town, in a drunken brawl that he'd probably started. And according to everyone in town, Carter was just like him. She resented her mother for putting that on him.

Those words cut to the quick, hitting her harder than Josie wanted to admit. But it was there, hanging between them. She'd never tell Deborah that she wasn't her real mother. She was. In every way that could matter, she was, except for one.

"If he's just like his daddy...Does that make me just like my biological parents? A terrified teenager and the soldier who raped her? What story is my blood telling?"

Deborah frowned. "I didn't mean it that way. It's just an expression, and I shouldn't have said it. No, it isn't just biology. The way you're raised has a lot to do with it."

"If that's the case, then there's no issue. Because Carter was never around his father, was he? You can't have it both ways, Mom."

Deborah rose. "I think I'll walk home. Clearly, this conversation is not going the way I intended...and I don't doubt that you've made other plans about where you're spending your evening. I trust you'll be discreet, Josephine. I don't need to tell you how the congregation would respond to the news that the pastor's daughter is cavorting with such a man."

"Do you even see me?" Josie asked.

"You're being melodramatic, Josephine. It's my fault for slapping such a name on you! Of course, I see you! What on earth kind of question is that?" Deborah demanded as she gathered her purse.

A valid one. For so many years, she'd wondered if

they adopted her because they really wanted *her* or if adopting a poor, unfortunate orphan from a war-torn country was just part of their overall package, like the mission trips to Haiti or feeding the homeless. She didn't feel like their daughter as much as she felt like a public work, an act of charity committed for the world to see.

If she said that, if she spoke those hateful words out loud, there'd be no taking them back. "Never mind. I'll be in church this Sunday. But I'm still not coming back to the choir. Daddy will just have to accept that."

Deborah nodded. "And Carter Hayes?"

"Some things are just my business and mine alone." Josie's tone was stiff, and the words firmer than she'd intended them to be.

It wasn't her mother who'd hurt her feelings. It was all her own doubts and fears creeping in, making her question her place in the world, making her question whether or not she really belonged there...or if she deserved the life that they'd given her.

Deborah's answering sigh echoed throughout the room. "Your father doesn't know about this. I don't intend to tell him. It isn't just that I don't approve of Carter. Certainly, he's made choices that are questionable, but many people have. You're my baby, Josie. The only one I'll ever have. I don't want to see you get your heart broken."

"I'm a big girl. I can handle it." Josie watched Deborah leave, the tension still high between them. When the door closed, she exhaled loudly. "I hope."

A glance at the clock showed her she didn't have much time. She'd told Carter she'd be there at seven, even though her heart wasn't really in it anymore. She felt hollowed out and miserable after the confrontation with her mother. Guilty. Her choices were letting them down, reflecting poorly on them. It was ridiculous.

Going upstairs, she changed quickly. There would be no naughty dress and killer heels. She donned a pair of frayed jeans and a University of Kentucky sweatshirt. If that wasn't hot enough for him, then he could just go to hell, she thought angrily. It wasn't even him she was pissed at.

"Get it together, Josie," she whispered softly. "Do not fuck this up. Right now, he's the only form of stress relief you have...and god, is he good at it."

Even as she said it, she felt like a horrible person. She was using him. She could see there was so much more to Carter Hayes than the fact that he had an amazing body and a mad set of skills to go with it.

In spite of his reputation, in spite of his admitted sleeping around, he was a good person. He didn't lie or cheat. He didn't say anything he didn't mean, and he never made a promise he didn't keep. Of course, that was easy enough to do when he simply avoided making promises altogether. Still, there was something to be said for that. He had his own sense of honor, his own code, and he followed it to the letter. Meanwhile, she was a huge hypocrite, pretending to be the good Christian girl her parents raised and slipping around with him at night.

Ignoring her attack of conscience, Josie grabbed her phone and keys and headed out the door. Some temptations were too great to resist. She'd make peace with her hypocrisy at some point. Until then, she just planned to keep herself distracted.

Six

I t was a quarter after. She'd stood him up. In his whole life, that had never happened. Not even once. It wasn't a feeling he cared for at all, not one bit.

"Son of a bitch," he muttered. Clicking the button on the remote, he turned the television off. He had no interest in the game, and he sure as hell wasn't going to sit around all night moping over the fact that she wasn't there.

Crossing the wide plank floors to his bedroom, he opened the closet door and retrieved a clean shirt. He'd go to the bar, have a few beers, and he wouldn't give that pint-sized pain in the ass a second thought.

The knock on the door stopped him cold. Shirt on, unbuttoned and hanging loose, he glanced at the clock beside the bed. She was almost half an hour late.

Pissed, he walked back into the living room and jerked the door open. She stood there wearing a sweatshirt that looked like it could have housed her three times over and the oldest, rattiest pair of jeans he'd ever seen. She still looked hot. Certainly hot enough to take the wind out of his sails.

"I didn't think you were coming," he said.

She shrugged. "I was having a few doubts myself."

Carter stepped back and allowed her inside. Somehow, he didn't think the evening was going to end the way he'd imagined. It felt shockingly like one of those we-need-to-talk moments that he always avoided.

"Well, I know it isn't because you didn't enjoy yourself last night. You did...several times, as a matter of fact."

"Can we skip the play-by-play?" she asked as she moved toward the couch. She sat down on the arm, crossed her arms over her chest, and looked utterly miserable.

Yes. It was definitely not going to go well. "Why don't you tell me whatever it is that's got you looking like a whipped pup? Guessing with women only ever causes trouble."

"My mom stopped by after work. Apparently, Doris called her this afternoon with her suspicions about your real reasons for stopping in the library."

Fuck. It had been an impulse. He didn't exactly regret his actions, but he did hate that they'd made problems for her. "I take it Mommy doesn't approve?"

"She has concerns...well-founded ones. I can't do this with you, Carter, if you don't take me seriously."

He shook his head. "I do take you seriously!"

"Then listen to me! When I tell you we can't be open about this thing between us...It's not just me that it affects. My parents, the church, my job at the library. Carter, I'm hanging by a thread there! Doris is looking for whatever reason she can find to get rid of me...and if she does, you know what happens? I have to move back into my parents' house! I can't do that, Carter. I can't give up the little bit of freedom I've managed to carve out for myself!"

She was shouting by the time she finished. Overwrought, as his grandmother would have said.

"I was just having a little fun today, Josie. I didn't mean for it to go so wrong for you. You can't keep living your life for other people."

She shook her head. "You don't understand. I wouldn't have a life at all if it weren't for these people. I won't embarrass them by dragging my name, the name they gave me, through the mud."

He didn't want to let her go. Eventually, yes. When he'd managed to get her out of his system, when the intense craving for her had passed, and he could think again. But not yet. Not now.

"What do you want from me, Josie? Just tell me."

A shrug and then a bitter laugh was her response. Finally, after a long pause, she spoke. "We both know we're not going anywhere with this. You're not the kind of guy who settles down. But I'm so tired of being the good girl for everybody...of not having anything for myself."

"Then don't be," he replied evenly. "Be whatever and whoever you want to be."

"I can't. I couldn't stand it if I disappointed them that way!"

It pissed him off that he would be the instrument of disappointment, that her being with him was in some way a failure.

"So you're just going to live a lonely, miserable, and disappointing life for yourself, then? 'Cause that makes perfect fucking sense!"

"Dammit, Carter. I didn't come here to fight with you!"

"Then what did you come here for?" he demanded.

"To feel the way I did last night."

"I guess that means I'm your dirty little secret." He uttered the words without heat, without any inflection at all, even though they stung his pride like being sliced by a thousand razors.

"If you don't want me on these terms, I can go," she replied. Her tone was equally devoid of inflection. It wasn't what either one of them wanted.

"Just so you know," he said, "I hate this fucking town and what it does to people. The expectations. The gossip. The miserable fucking people who sit back in their tidy little houses and judge everyone else...I hate it."

She'd never voiced those thoughts. Like so many things that ran through her mind, it just created feelings of guilt and shame. Her life could be so much worse. But no one would ever let her forget that.

"So do I. But I don't have anywhere else to go." Admitting it made her feel weak and breathless, as fearful as if an angry, pitchfork-wielding mob was outside the door. "I don't want this to end yet. I know it will eventually, but not yet, Carter. Can't we just enjoy it for now?"

"You want a hot, steamy, secret affair? I'll give you one," he vowed.

Carter didn't waste another second. He moved toward her, grabbing her ponytail and tugging her head back. He kissed the side of her neck, his teeth scraping over her skin with just enough force, just enough of a bite to make her moan and shiver. His mouth roamed over her. Lips, teeth, tongue.

He didn't mark her skin, but the urge to do so was there. A part of him wanted to mark her, to show the world that she was his. Instead, he grabbed the hem of her sweatshirt and jerked it upward and over her head, tossing it aside until he could close one hand on the soft mound of her breast. Through her bra, he could feel the hard peak of her nipple.

Josie's head fell back against him, and a soft cry escaped her. Lips parted, eyes closed, her cheeks flushed with passion. That was how he wanted her. He tugged her head back just a bit further, his hand fisted in her hair. She was in charge of some things, he thought, but not everything.

"Carter," she gasped, clutching at his hand.

"You want this to be a secret...how quiet can you be, Josie?" he whispered against her ear. "When I'm touching you this way, tasting you...or when I'm inside you?"

"Carter, please," she murmured, her hand covering his, pressing his palm against her breast. "I can't think when you're doing that."

"Then don't, baby. Just feel. Feel all the ways I can make you burn."

He was relentless. His hands roamed over her freely, touching her everywhere as he continued to kiss her neck, her shoulders. Nipping at her earlobes with his teeth, he savored the startled cry that escaped her and the shiver that followed.

Carter let go of her hair, but her head stayed back, resting against his shoulder, arching of her own accord to give him free access. His hand skimmed along the indentation of her spine, down to the waistband of her jeans, sliding beneath them. His fingers traced the lacy pattern of her thong, brushing lightly over her skin as she clung to him.

"Tell me you want me, Josie," he commanded.

"I do. Oh god, I do," she sobbed. "You're killing me, Carter."

Carter pulled back and hauled her up from the arm of

the couch until she was perched on the back of it. With one hand, he unsnapped and unzipped her jeans. Within seconds, he had them tugged down her legs, pulling them and her sneakers off in one swift movement. She wore only a lacy bra and an equally lacy thong.

"Why do I always wind up naked first?" she asked.

"'Cause you're little and easier to strip," Carter replied. He wasn't taking her to his bed. She wanted hot and steamy, and he was going to give it to her. She wanted it to feel like a tawdry affair? Well, he would provide all that she asked for and more.

He grasped the elastic band of her thong, but rather than sliding it over her hips, he twisted it around his fingers, tugging, until the whole thing simply snapped. Tossing the scrap of fabric aside, he pressed her back, her body balanced on the cushions of the sofa, her head tilted back, and her legs locked around his waist. He unzipped his own pants, dug a condom from his wallet, and rolled it on quickly.

Sinking into her, feeling the heat of her closing around him, he gripped her hips tighter. His fingers dug into the soft flesh there as she closed around him like a fist. He bit back a groan as he surged into her. Christ almighty, nothing had ever felt that good.

Pumping his hips, thrusting into her again and again as she sobbed beneath him, Carter knew he wasn't going to let her go. Not for a good long time.

He felt her thighs tense, the muscles drawing so taut they quivered. Her breathing changed, and a flush crept over her pale skin. She was hovering right there on the edge, ready to come for him.

"You're mine, Josie. For as long as I want you," he vowed.

He felt the shudder ripple through her as her body

clenched around him. The low, keening cry as she shivered beneath him was the sweetest sound he'd ever heard. Carter stopped holding back, stopped trying to keep his own need in check. He drove into her again—deeper, harder—drawing out her pleasure even as he gave into his own.

Josie couldn't breathe. Somehow, they'd migrated from the back of the couch and were lying cuddled together on it, covered with a chenille blanket that was a decidedly feminine touch in his otherwise masculine abode. It was best not to think about where that blanket had come from. It would only piss her off. Being jealous over him was a waste of time and energy. Every woman in town had either wanted him, had him, or planned to try.

Carter had pulled her tighter, pressing her face against his chest until she couldn't even draw breath. Managing to turn her head, Josie pushed against him until he mumbled in his sleep. Even then, barely conscious, his hand cupped her breast and squeezed gently.

She rolled her eyes. "Carter, wake up!"

He grumbled again, but made no move to let her up. Finally, out of desperation, Josie reached over and grabbed his chest hair, giving it a hard tug.

"Ow!" he shouted, eyes flying open. "What the hell did you do that for?"

"Because I need to pee, and you sleep like the damn dead. Let me up!"

Carter murmured under his breath, something that was undoubtedly a string of curse words. But he did manage to roll to a sitting position, allowing her to climb over top of him and off the couch.

After attending to nature's call, Josie stood there in front of the sink, washing her hands and taking in her reflection. She looked like a wild woman. Her hair was a mess, her makeup smeared. She had beard burn on her cheeks and chin. But she looked *alive*, like something had finally just lit up inside her.

For the longest time, she'd just been going through the motions. Clean the house. Go to work. Come home. Go to church. Do, as always, what everyone says because it would appear ungrateful not to. Somehow or other, her life had become nothing more than an expression of gratitude to her parents. The realization weighed heavily on her. But for now, it appeared things were changing dramatically.

She didn't know if it was Carter. Maybe it was just rebellion, maybe it was the thrill of having a secret that no one knew for sure, even if a few did suspect. Or maybe it was just hot, amazing sex that left her knees weak. Whatever it was, it felt good. *She* felt good. And she didn't want to give that up.

Leaving the bathroom, she saw that he'd moved from the couch to the bed.

"I should go," she said lamely. It wasn't what she wanted. If she were to do what she wanted, she'd crawl into that bed with him, snuggle against his chest while he held her and rubbed her back until they both fell asleep. And of course, in the morning, they'd have more amazing, mind-blowing sex.

"You can stay," he said.

He didn't tell her he wanted her to. He didn't ask her to. Instead, he left it totally in her court. She wanted him to demand it, she realized. Some perverse part of her wanted him to be the one putting his pride on the line instead of hers.

"We both have to work tomorrow," she protested. "And if anyone saw me—yeah. That's not a good idea."

Grabbing her discarded clothes in the living room, Josie dressed quickly. Her panties were a lost cause. Between the pair he'd stolen from her and the pair he'd destroyed, the man was playing hell on her lingerie budget. As Josie slipped her sneakers back on, he emerged from the bedroom wearing just a pair of jeans, only partially fastened. He wore nothing beneath them. Her eyes followed the line of hair that bisected his perfectly defined abs only to disappear behind denim that looked so damn good on him it made her want to cry.

"I'll see you this weekend," he said. "At your house."

"That is not a good idea," she said.

"Relax. I've got it all worked out," he offered with a wink.

"That is the least reassuring thing I have ever heard anyone say." Josie didn't want him working things out. She wanted things like they were. Sneaking around like two grounded teenagers was working for her. Some inner kinky bitch that she'd never known about was actually kind of enjoying it.

"Your privacy fence is falling apart. It won't make it through the winter," he explained. "Naturally, you're not going to be out there fixing it yourself. Hiring a handy-man, Josie, is your only option...and after I repair the fence, then we can discuss payment."

"Payment?" she asked. "Really? Now I'm supposed to pimp myself for home repair?"

"It's really good home repair," he promised. "It'll be mutually beneficial. In fact, I'll guarantee that and the fence."

She felt herself caving. All of her protests collapsing under the weight of his wicked grin and the knowledge that he was absolutely right.

"You do realize we're crazy, right? That there's no way whatever we're doing is going to end well?" she asked.

His expression grew shuttered, the teasing light leaving his eyes. For a moment, just for a split second, she thought maybe she'd hurt him. But then she dismissed the thought. She was a diversion for him, heretofore unconquered territory. Women were disposable to Carter. They always had been and always would. If she let herself think any differently, she'd wind up brokenhearted for sure.

"Why are you borrowing trouble, Josie?" he asked softly.

"Just stating the obvious. You'll get tired of me. Or I'll get tired of you. The odds of us getting tired of each other at exactly the same time and walking away on good terms? Yeah, those are pretty damn slim."

He shook his head. "You can't control everything, Josie. I don't know where this is going, but I'll be damned if I'm going to spend every minute of the time we have together anticipating the end."

She had hurt him, she realized, stunned that she even possessed the power to do so. At the very least, she'd nicked his pride. "I don't mean to be difficult...But I have to protect myself, Carter. I don't want to get my heart broken."

"I'm not an asshole, Josie! I don't make promises and then bail on them," he said defensively. "I've never been anything but honest with any of the women I've dated."

She shook her head sadly. He didn't understand, but then he wouldn't.

"For all that, for all the women that just fall at your feet, you don't understand us at all. You don't have to lie to us, Carter. We lie to ourselves. We build these elaborate fantasies in our heads of how things will work out. We plan weddings and houses and babies...There's a whole universe of expectation tied up in nothing more than a first date. So when I say this is going to end, I'm not saying it because of you, Carter. I'm just reminding myself to stay focused on what's here and now, and not what I want it to be down the road."

He didn't respond, just stared at her like she'd started speaking in tongues, and he didn't have an interpreter present. Josie grabbed her keys and marched toward the door. She wasn't mad at him, but she was more than a little mad at herself.

It was all well and good to talk about keeping her distance, of reminding herself that theirs was a finite arrangement, but it didn't stop the flare of hope in her. It certainly didn't do anything to lessen the fact that all she wanted, more than anything else in the world at that moment, was to be curled up in his arms. If ever there was a reason to turn tail and run, that was it.

She needed space, she needed perspective, and she needed to find some way to armor herself against the hurt that was going to come crashing down sooner or later.

After Josie left, Carter stared at the door for the longest time. She tied him up in fucking knots, he thought bitterly as he walked into the kitchen to grab a beer. It was perverse to want her, an exercise in misery since she was clearly the most prickly, contrary, and difficult woman who'd ever walked the face of the earth.

Using the antique bottle opener mounted to the wall,

he popped the lid off the beer. He didn't actually want to drink it. He didn't want to sit around in his apartment and mope about her. Putting the bottle in the sink, he grabbed his discarded shirt from earlier, then put on his boots.

Heading out into the night, his aimless drive wound up taking him to the farm. The lights were on in the barn, so he knew Emmitt would be up. Letting himself in, he drove right up the open doors of the barn and then climbed out of the truck.

There was no telling what he would find inside. As the local vet, Emmitt tended to keep a lot of sick or injured animals in the barn if they couldn't be treated at their home or fit in the exam rooms of the attached clinic.

But it wasn't an animal emergency that had Emmitt out there so late. He was putting down fresh straw in the stalls.

"You do realize that it's almost midnight," Carter pointed out.

"You do realize that if you want to talk, you better be willing to work," Emmitt said and tossed the pitchfork toward him.

Carter caught it by the handle and sighed. He should have stayed home. Still, he walked over and started spreading the straw. It was hard work, burning the muscles, but soothing the mind.

"So why are you out cruising around in the middle of the night?" Emmitt finally asked.

"My evening didn't go as planned."

"Her husband came home early?" Emmitt shot back.

"You're not funny," Carter said. "I don't mess with married women...that I know of."

"If it's midnight, and you're in my barn instead of someone's bed, there's a problem." Emmitt shot back.

Carter finished spreading the straw in the stall and went for another bale. Hoisting it onto his shoulder, he carried it over and set it down, using a pocket knife to snap the twine that bound it. "Let's just say we move in different circles...There's some conflict there."

"Church lady?"

Carter frowned. "How do you figure?"

Emmitt laughed, a rusty sound that was rarely ever heard. "That's the only circle you don't run in. Either step up or step off, Carter. If you want her, you have to meet her where she is...and if you're not willing to do that, let her go."

Yeah. He wasn't going to church with Josie. He wasn't going to sit there in the front row under the disapproving eye of her daddy. That shit was not happening.

"You give shitty advice, Emmitt."

"I give good advice that you don't like. Now shut up and spread that straw. I'd like to get to bed sometime before daylight."

"Why the hell are you up doing this right now, anyway?"

Emmitt lifted another bale and carried it back to the larger of the stalls. "Had an emergency earlier today. Horse broke its leg. Had to put it down. Old man Jeffers... Between his bad hips and his dementia, I couldn't leave him to handle it. So I borrowed a backhoe and got one of the neighbors to help me with it. Took all damn day."

Emmitt Hayes, the Surly Saint, Carter thought with a bitter laugh. "Half the town thinks you're a hateful bastard, and the other half thinks the pope should be knocking on your door."

"He's a hundred damn years old. He could break a hip looking at that damn backhoe. What was I supposed to do?" Emmitt demanded.

Carter didn't say anything else. Just spread straw in the various stalls. Emmitt was just as locked down by what people in Fontaine thought as the rest of them were. That didn't make his current situation any clearer, though.

Feeling his muscles burning from slinging the pitchfork around and feeling the bite of the handle in his hands, he realized he probably should have just stayed home and drunk the beer.

Seven

J osie listened to the hum of power tools as she stood upstairs in her bedroom. True to his word, Carter had shown up with a load of wood and his tools and was out back repairing her privacy fence. Meanwhile, she was upstairs trying to figure out what to wear to seduce him when he came inside. Of course, he didn't require a whole lot of seduction, but it felt good to dress for him, to put something on her body just so he'd have the pleasure of stripping it off her.

The idea of having him in her bedroom was strange. She'd never had any man in her bedroom, period. Other than a few painfully inept encounters in her dorm room at college, and then the boy she'd dated her last year at UK who only wished he could be called a minuteman, she'd never had men in her space. Certainly never a man like Carter, who seemed to leave his mark on everything.

The backyard grew silent, the hum of power tools faded, the soft thump of the hammer was gone. Josie reached into the drawer and retrieved a black nightie that she'd bought on impulse and never worn. The silk slithered over her skin, falling to the middle of her thighs. The deep V in the front was supported by the thinnest spaghetti straps in creation, but the back dipped even lower. It barely covered her ass from above or below.

She ran the brush through her hair just as she heard the back door open. Moving to the bed, Josie had intended to arrange herself in an alluring pose, but Carter had taken the stairs quicker than she expected. She was on her knees in the middle of the bed when she heard his low whistle.

"You've been holding out on me," he said. "That's enough to give a man a heart attack."

"Maybe you should come closer in case I need to give you CPR?" she shot back.

"I need a shower first," he said. "I'm disgusting."

All she could think about was Carter naked in her shower, water pouring down over his tanned skin. God above.

"Bathroom is through there," she said, pointing to one of the doors just across the hall. "But the only soap I have smells like roses."

He walked toward her, kissed her hard on the mouth, and as he pulled back, said with a grin, "I've smelled like worse things. Do not move from this spot, Josie Marcum. I'm going to get cleaned up, and when I come back in here, I'm going to show you just how dirty I can be."

It was a damn good thing she was on the bed already because when he said that, her knees would have buckled. The heat of his gaze and the sensual promise of his words had all but laid her low.

Carter disappeared across the hall, and Josie flopped back on the bed. He'd told her to wait, but the temptation of him wet and naked was more than she could bear. The second the shower turned on and she heard the rings of the shower curtain sliding closed, her decision was made.

Climbing from the bed, Josie opened the bathroom door and stepped inside. Carter's clothes were on the floor. She stepped over them as she stripped the nightie off.

"I told you to wait for me," he said, his voice carrying over the sound of the water.

"I thought we'd have more fun in here," she replied, opening the curtain just enough to step into the tub behind him.

Carter turned and rinsed the shampoo from his hair. He reached for her bottle of conditioner, and she smirked at him.

"What?" he demanded.

"If I wasn't staring at ever-growing proof to the contrary, Carter, I'd swear you were a girl."

"It makes my hair feel nice," he said simply. "And you like my hair, so don't even pretend you mind."

She did like his hair, and just about everything else about him. In that, she was totally caught. That didn't mean she was going to feed his gargantuan ego, though.

"But if you ask to use my flat iron, it's a deal breaker. Clear?"

"If I ask for your flat iron," he said, as he worked the conditioner through his hair, "Then you can just take my balls as payment. They'd be useless to me after that, anyway."

When he was done with his hair, he pulled her close, plastering her to him and spun them around. The spray was warmer than she'd expected, and she let out a squeak.

"Too hot?" he asked.

"I'll get used to it," she said.

When her hair was completely saturated, Carter

turned her again so that her back was to his chest. He squeezed some of her shampoo into his palm and began to work a lather into her hair. He didn't just wash her hair. He massaged her scalp, his hands kneading and easing knots of tension she hadn't even been aware existed. He rubbed her temples and then the tender spot just behind her ears, working his way down to her neck.

"Oh, sweet lord. I feel like I'm melting," she said.

Carter grinned. "Then I'm doing it right."

She leaned against him, practically unable to support her own weight. He rinsed the shampoo from her hair, then applied a liberal amount of conditioner and repeated the whole process.

If anyone had told her that having a man wash her hair for her would be one of the most erotic experiences of her life, she would have thought they were crazy. But then, she was naked in the shower with Carter, and it would be impossible for it to be anything less. She heard his name, she thought about sex. She saw him, she thought about sex. He touched her, and she wanted to climb him.

With her hair rinsed clean, her head resting against his chest, Carter tugged her closer. She could feel the hard ridge of his erection pressed against her. Her body responded accordingly. The rush of heat between her thighs was intense and instant.

His hands moved from her neck down to her shoulders, then slipped lower. They coasted up and down her back in soft, slow strokes that left her shivering before sliding around her waist and then back up to cup her breasts. His fingers closed over her nipples, squeezing just a shade beyond gentle, leaving her gasping.

"I want you all the time," he said, whispering against her ear. "I wake up thinking about you...I go to bed thinking about you. The way you smell. The way you taste. You drive me crazy."

She wanted to answer, to tell him that he drove her crazy too. But she couldn't think, much less form words, with his hands on her, with his body pressed against her.

His hands continued to roam—kneading, caressing, teasing. If he hadn't been supporting her weight entirely, she would simply have collapsed into a puddle at his feet.

"Carter, I feel like I all I ever do is beg you to hurry... but dammit, hurry!" she said.

Josie felt him grin against her neck, just before he nipped that same tender spot with his teeth. "You have to learn to be patient, cupcake. The longer you wait for it, the better it feels."

She started to respond, but a noise from outside made her heart literally drop to her feet. The garage door was opening.

"Someone's here!"

Carter sighed as he stepped back from her. "Which window do I need to climb out of?" The note of disappointment and anger in his voice was impossible to miss.

"None of them! You just have to hide!" she hissed.

"Where?" he demanded.

"Just stay here," she said. "No one has any reason to come up here to the bathroom."

He looked at her like she'd lost her mind. "I'm just supposed to stand here in the shower and wait for you to get rid of whoever it is? Did you forget that my truck is parked outside?"

"I'll lie," she said decisively. "I'll tell them that Bennett picked you up to help him move something, and you're coming back for it later."

He frowned at her then. "You came up with that really quick. Been planning what you'd say for a while?"

There was something in his tone that told her he wasn't playing. He was pissed. Really pissed.

"Carter, the only people who have the code for the garage are my parents and my grandmother. It sure as hell isn't Nana back from Florida. I can't tell them you're here!"

"No. Of course, you can't," he agreed reasonably.

Carter was never reasonable. "I don't know what you want me to say," she said lamely.

"I want you to say that you're not ashamed to be seen with me. But we both know that's not going to happen. I might not have a lot, Josie, but I do have some pride, and I don't think I'm gonna let you take it from me."

"I can't fight about this with you right now! They'll be inside any second!" She didn't even want to think about the kind of disaster that would result from her father finding a naked Carter Hayes in her house.

"We're not fighting about it, Josie. Just go. See your parents."

Josie got out of the shower, and he turned the water off. He stepped out behind her, and she handed him a towel. He took it without a word and began to dry his hair. It wasn't just his pride. She'd thought that at first, but she could see it in his eyes. She was hurting him when it never even dawned on her that she had the power to.

"Carter—" She stopped, unsure of what to say to him. It didn't change anything for her. She was still the daughter of the most upstanding minister in town, and everything she said and did still reflected on him and the church. And Carter was so much more than anyone realized, including her, but in a town like Fontaine, that would never matter.

"Just go," he said.

Josie grabbed a robe from the back of the door and

headed across the hall to dress. Sweatpants and an ancient T-shirt on, she headed down the stairs where her parents were standing at the kitchen door surveying the work in the back.

"You didn't have to hire Carter Hayes to fix the fence, Josie," her father said. "I would have done it for you."

"He gave me a really good price," she lied. It felt wrong. Everything about it felt wrong.

"Well, it doesn't look right," her mother said. It was clear from Deborah's sharp gaze that she *knew*. This clearly didn't jibe with her earlier admonishment to be discreet. She could see from her mother's rigid posture and cold gaze that Deborah was livid. "That boy's truck parked in front of your house will cause talk, Josephine."

Josie stiffened. "What does it matter? People will talk if they want to talk, either about me or about someone else. I hate all the gossip and judgment. You should too," she said accusingly. "Maybe you need to write a sermon about people minding their own business?"

William Marcum frowned at her. "Do not speak to your mother that way, Josephine!"

"Don't come into my house and tell me what I should and shouldn't do when I'm a grown woman," she shot back. "I'm not a child. I'm entitled to live my life without your interference!"

Deborah drew back as if she'd been slapped. "I can't believe you'd speak to us this way, Josephine. After everything we've done for you!"

Josie felt it then. The guilt and the shame crawled beneath her skin, and the whispered words of every single member of her father's congregation echoed in her mind.

You're so lucky they took you in. You should be so grateful they saved you. Where would you be if God hadn't called them to open their home to a poor orphan?

71

But for the first time, there was anger with the guilt. Anger that what should have been done out of love had been reduced to a currency to control her.

Her voice quivered as she spoke. The anger and the hurt, not to mention the resentment that had been building for years, were all bubbling just below the surface, like a volcano ready to explode.

"You have done a lot for me. And I've never been anything but grateful...but that doesn't mean I have to live my entire life trying to earn your love and acceptance. You both need to leave."

William stepped forward. "Your mother didn't mean it that way, Josie. We're lucky to have you, and we both know it. There is nothing you could ever do that would make us think differently."

He meant that, or at least he believed he did. But if they really felt that way, wouldn't they have said so before? During all the conversations where she stood there beside them after church, and people praised them for taking her in and raising her like their own, wouldn't they have said then that she was their own?

"Then maybe you should have told the congregation that. All I've heard my whole life is how you sacrificed, how you gave up so much for me...I'm a burden. I'm proof of your Christian duty and nothing more."

"That's not true. We've never made you feel that way!" Deborah protested.

"You just did!" Josie protested. "But more to the point, you never once tried to stop everyone else from making me feel that way."

The tension in the room was so thick it could be cut with a knife. The silence stretched between them, growing heavier by the second.

Finally, William said, "We'll go. We just wanted to

make sure you were okay. But you're clearly upset and us being here isn't making it better."

It was a peace offering of sorts, but she didn't want it. She didn't want to be placated and made to feel like she was being humored or patronized. She had a right to feel the things she did.

"No, it really isn't...and which one of my neighbors is your spy? Or is it the whole damned street?"

Her father looked at her in a way that made her feel petty and small. "Watch your language. I understand that you're upset, and yes, one of your neighbors called, but they were concerned about you. If Carter Hayes is in this house, it's abundantly clear you want him to be, so we'll go."

Josie watched them leave and immediately wondered what she'd done. She'd yelled at her parents. Not even as a crazy ass, hormonal teenager had she spoken so sharply to her mother. She'd been mean, petty, and spiteful. She'd rebelled against them.

"Oh god. Oh god. Oh god." She just kept muttering the phrase over and over again, shocked at her own behavior and terrified that she'd ruined things forever.

After a few minutes, Carter came down the stairs. His wet hair was slicked back, and he'd dressed in the same clothes he'd discarded earlier. He didn't look mad anymore. He looked...resigned.

"I'm going to go," he said.

"What?" Josie couldn't make sense of what was happening inside her, much less what anyone else was saying to her. She felt sick, scared, and like her whole world had just tilted.

"I'm going. You're not in any kind of condition for whatever we were going to do earlier. And you need to get yourself cleaned up and go over to your parents," he added.

"Why would I go there?"

He walked over to her and pulled her against him. In a surprisingly tender gesture, he kissed the top of her head. "Because if you don't, you're going to worry about it all night. Apologize to them. Let them apologize to you."

"What about you? I owe you an apology too," she said, and tried to choke back a sob.

"You don't owe me anything. I can swallow my pride for a while longer, Josie. My ego's pretty healthy. It can take it."

She was still crying, but that did pull a soft laugh from her. "You're better than people believe you are, Carter. And you're better than I deserve."

He wasn't. But until she figured out just what she was worth, it wouldn't do a damn bit of good to tell her that.

"Take a few days and let things calm down. Let people find something else to gossip about...and then we'll embark on illicit affair part two."

Carter left, heading out to his truck. Climbing behind the wheel, he sat there for a moment. It wasn't what he wanted, but he'd take what he could get. The only other option was to walk away altogether, and he wasn't ready for that yet.

His knuckles were white on the steering wheel, and his whole body was tense with the combination of hurt, anger, and unslaked lust. There was only one option. Liquor.

Eight

Carter settled back onto the couch at Bennett's house and dug his hand into a bag of chips. Nothing but dust. He lifted the bag and dumped the remainder directly into his mouth. Bennett had been slacking on groceries ever since Mia Darcy had come back into the picture. But that was apparently done now, or it was if Bennett's mood was any indication. He'd been a dick all day long.

Taking a long pull from his beer, he emptied the dregs from the bottle. It was disgusting. Bennett's was still sitting on the coffee table, so Carter grabbed it and drained what was left in the bottle, washing down the last of the crumbs. Much better, he thought.

He knew it was gross. He knew he'd been moping around just as much as Bennett, but he'd be damned if he'd let anyone else see it.

Bennett came back into the living room and flopped down on the couch. The game was on. It was going to shit, but it was on. Basketball season would turn everything around, Carter thought. Unable to watch the disgrace, Carter rose to his feet and walked out onto the porch. The rain had just started. Tilting his head back, he inhaled the scent of it.

He fucking missed her. He missed the way she giggled when he tickled her belly, the way she smelled, the way she snuggled against him in bed. God, he was a sad-ass bastard, he thought. It had been just over a week, but all he did was think about her. He didn't know if that was enough time for the Fontaine gossip mill to shut down or change gears, but it was all the damn time he was giving them.

Taking his phone from his pocket, he glanced at the last text from Josie. It had come two days earlier, and he hadn't replied. He'd told her he could swallow his pride, but he just wasn't sure if that was true. It stung like a bitch.

It would be different if she were just another fling, but she wasn't. Of course, it wouldn't matter what he said to her. She wouldn't believe it. The only thing that would make her believe it was time. And he was back to square one, because giving her time would mean swallowing his pride.

Fuck it, he decided, and started tapping out a message on the keypad.

> I want to see you.

He didn't expect an immediate response. In fact, he expected her to be so pissed she might not respond at all. While he'd been pouting, and he was man enough to admit that's what it was, she'd been left hanging in the wind.

On the one hand, he understood her completely. Every word she'd said to her parents that day in the kitchen had carried up the stairs to him. Feeling the weight of judgment from everyone in town on your back was something he understood on a fundamental level. He'd been living that way all his life. Every time someone said to him that he was just like his father, it meant one thing. He'd come to a bad end.

Josie was broken inside. It didn't matter that she looked whole and pristine on the outside. Inside, she was still a scared little girl who didn't believe that good things would last.

His phone dinged. Looking down at the screen, grinned.

> You took your damned time.

Carter smiled. If she texted him back that quickly, it meant he wasn't totally screwed. She'd make him pay. That was her nature, but he wasn't sure he minded. Watching her get worked up and pissed off was one of life's greatest joys, as far as he was concerned. Thoughts like that would have made him panic at one point in time. He didn't get attached, but from the moment she'd thrown that first shoe at him, everything with Josie had been different.

Carter heard Bennett cursing from inside. He'd discovered he was out of beer. He started to turn and go back into the house, to face the music and to bust Bennett's balls a little, but through the rain, he saw something that stopped him.

Mia Darcy was walking down the road, barefoot, and she looked like hell. Something was very, very wrong.

"Bennett!"

He could hear Bennett curse from inside the house. "What the hell do you want?"

"Bennett! Get your ass out here! Now!"

Bennett appeared in the doorway. "What the fuck is it?"

Carter ignored his shitty mood and pointed to the disheveled woman walking down the driveway. "You've got company."

Carter stood back as Bennett crossed the expanse of the porch and headed into the yard. He looked at Mia, really looked at her. The girl looked broken, like maybe all the pieces would never go together again. But he also saw the way Bennett held onto her. Whatever was between them, whatever ugly history and hurt feelings, they had something that defied all of it.

For just a second, Carter was jealous. What would it take for Josie to come to him that way? She wouldn't, he realized. There was nothing, as far as he could figure, that would ever be as important to her as the way this town saw her.

The wind picked up, and the rain that had been falling straight down slashed inward, plastering his shirt to him. The cold hit him like a knife. Another glance at Mia and he realized she was absolutely blue with cold, but whatever she was saying to Bennett seemed to be more important than getting warm.

Carter stepped inside the house and grabbed a blanket off the couch. Carrying it into the yard, he passed it to Bennett and watched him wrap it around Mia as she stood there tearfully confessing everything.

He didn't hear it all, just enough to know that Samuel Darcy was as big a bastard as he'd always thought he was, and then some. Not wanting to intrude and feeling more than a little uncomfortable with the whole situation, Carter retreated to the house.

In the kitchen, he hopped up on the counter and

checked his phone again. There was another text from Josie.

> That's it? I want to see you and then radio silence?

Carter thought about for a second before replying, just trying to get his thoughts in order.

> Shit hit the fan. Mia Darcy is here. In full view of everyone. I'll come to your house after dark. Leave the back door unlocked.

There was a pause of about two heartbeats and then those damned annoying dots on the screen as he waited for her reply. Her saying yay or nay seemed like a life and death decision.

> You're telling me every detail when you get here.

It didn't escape him that she was more interested in what was going on with Bennett and Mia than with whatever was happening with them. Good god, but she was hell on his ego.

> Fine.

After typing the single word response, he pressed the send key. Getting up from the counter, he opened the cabinets until he found one lonely bag of chips stuffed behind everything. Savannah had probably hidden them the last time she was there.

Contraband in hand, Carter returned to the living

room and the rest of the sad-ass game. Bennett had taken Mia upstairs, and he was just going to hang out until he knew he wasn't needed. And eat the rest of Bennett's chips.

It was a good ten minutes before Bennett came back downstairs. He took one look at Carter, who was elbow deep in a bag of corn chips, and grimaced. "You dickhead."

"Hey," Carter said, making to get up off the couch. The last thing he wanted was to hang around them and be reminded that his own love life was in the toilet. "I'm just getting out of your way."

Love life. Where the hell had that thought come from, he wondered? Sex life. Yes. He'd been having a very active one of those for a decade plus, and he was all about that. But love was something else.

Did he love Josie? No, he thought. Not yet. But he could. Easily. She'd just have to give him half a chance.

"Don't. I need you to stay here with Mia while I take care of something," Bennett said.

Panic hit Carter squarely in the chest. "No. Oh, hell no. I do not deal with crying women."

Bennett rolled his eyes. "You made that pretty clear by running like a whipped dog at the sight of her!"

It hadn't been the crying that sent him running. Looking at Bennett and Mia together, in an intimate moment that was not at all about being physical, that was just a little closer than he wanted to be to either of them. But it also reminded him of just how fucked up his own situation was.

"I got her a blanket. That was sensitive."

Bennett closed his eyes and pinched the bridge of his nose just the way their grandfather had always done when one of them was being an idiot. "That was first aid, you dumb fuck!"

"How long?" Carter asked, thinking about the texts from Josie. He needed to go there. He needed to see her. Standing her up wouldn't go well for either of them.

"I don't know. An hour. Maybe two. She's going to sleep like the dead. She'll never even know I left."

He could do that. It would put him late getting to her, but he'd text her and let her know. "Fine. But you owe me."

"You've been paid in chips and beer," Bennett called back as he grabbed his keys and headed out.

"The chips are stale," Carter said under his breath. Settling deeper into the couch, he pulled out his phone and glanced at the picture of Josie that he'd snapped while she wasn't looking. Wearing a UK sweatshirt and a smile, it cut him right to the quick.

"I'm a fucking idiot," he said aloud. "And this little girl is going to ruin me."

Even as he uttered the words, he knew they were the truth. But he was still having a hard time caring.

Nine

J osie glanced at the clock. He'd texted her back and told her was running late. But it was nearly ten, and she'd nearly given up. Rolling onto her side, she stared out the window.

Yes, she was curious about Bennett and Mia. Who wouldn't be? The whole town was on tenterhooks, waiting to see what was going to happen with them. But more than anything, she just wanted Carter there telling her the story. He wasn't always sympathetic to Mia, but she understood that. His loyalty would always lie with Bennett, as it should.

She heard the back door open and let out a sigh of relief. A part of her had wondered if he'd changed his mind. She wouldn't blame him. There was a part of her that wanted to throw caution to the wind and tell her parents and everyone else in town exactly what he meant to her. But then she'd have to admit it to both herself and Carter, and that terrified her.

Carter wasn't known for sticking. In fact, the minute any woman had started to cling, he'd run like the wind.

She didn't want to be *that girl*, and she didn't want to corner him and make him be *that guy*. So it was back to being a chicken and sticking with the status quo as long as they could manage it.

She sat up in bed, propped on her hands as the door opened.

"Hey," she said lamely. It wasn't exactly the sexiest of greetings.

"Hey," he said in return. It was awkward for both of them. Neither of them had spoken since the scene in the kitchen with her parents, other than the few texts they'd exchanged.

But there was one thing she had to say before anything else happened. She had to get it out.

"I'm sorry."

"For what?"

She shrugged. "For being a brat. For being too much of a chickenshit to just live my life. For being so worried about what other people might think of me that it leaves me all but paralyzed. Do I need to go on?"

He sat down on the edge of the bed, facing her, but leaving at least an arm's length between them. Which was never good. If Carter wanted to talk, she was pretty sure the only thing he'd be saying was goodbye.

"You don't need to apologize to me for that," he said. "Does it sting my pride? Hell, of course it does. But the thing about it is, Josie, you're right."

"Excuse me?"

He chuckled. "People in this town will judge you. They will be all up in your business. I saw Mia and Bennett together tonight, and I got it. For the first time, I really got just how much he loves her. And how much she loves him. But this fucking town, and all the busybodies in it, her father included, nearly destroyed that."

83

She didn't know what to say to that, so she remained silent. He was quiet, too, thinking. When he did speak again, he made her an offer that she hadn't seen coming.

"So we'll do this your way. Secret. I'll sneak in and out of your house at night when you want me here. You don't have to worry about being seen coming and going by your nosy-ass neighbors...and if you learn to stifle your screams a little bit, no one will be the wiser."

"For how long?" It wouldn't end well. She knew that, but there was no possible way it could. She might as well enjoy it for as long as she could.

"Until it stops being fun for either one of us," he said.

"We're not exactly having fun now," she said.

His cocky smile was enough to melt the panties right off her. "We could be."

He didn't need to make the offer twice. Reaching for the hem of her T-shirt, Josie pulled it up and over her head, and then tossed it to the corner of the room.

"Shut up then, and show me."

He laughed. "You're not the boss of me, Josie Marcum," he said, throwing her own inebriated words back at her.

"I don't have any shoes to throw at you right now," she protested. "Are you ever going to do something with that mouth that isn't talking?"

He pulled back the covers, exposing her legs and the simple cotton panties she wore. She'd thought about changing, about putting on something slinky and sexy. But she'd done that last time, and it had been an unmitigated disaster. Also, it smacked of trying too hard. Of expectation.

Carter crawled up the bed, his arms caging her, his weight pressing her back. She was used to feeling short, but being so close to him, she felt small and delicate, feminine and vulnerable in a way that both terrified and excited her.

"You call the shots outside of this room," he said. "You wanted secret? I'll give it to you. But in here, Josephine, I'm in charge. We clear?"

A shudder rippled through her. They were perfectly clear, and he'd never been hotter. She couldn't speak, so she just nodded.

He smiled as he pressed a kiss against her chest, his tongue gliding over the delicate skin between her breasts. With Carter, it was like her entire body became an erogenous zone. He could touch her anywhere, and it was instant heat.

She didn't try to rush him. She knew better. Carter was going to do what Carter wanted to do and when he wanted to do it. Her only option was to tell him to stop or to let him drive her completely insane with lust.

His hands roamed her skin, callused fingertips grazing, dragging over sensitive flesh until she was writhing beneath him. Everywhere his hands traveled, his mouth followed. Hot, open-mouthed kisses, the nip of his teeth driving her to the edge. She hovered there, her body drawn as taut as a bowstring. Tension coiled in her. Her breath came in sharp pants. And all she wanted was to feel him inside her, to have him ease the unbearable ache that he'd created.

When he finally rose and stripped off his own clothes, baring his perfect body to her, Josie couldn't not touch him. Sliding her hands over his steely thighs, her nails raking his skin and eliciting a sharp hiss from him, she smiled.

"You're in charge. If you don't want me to do this..."

He didn't tell her no, but he did grip her wrist and move her hand exactly where he wanted. With his hand over hers, he closed her fingers around him, guiding her, showing her exactly what he wanted. Stroking him, feeling him growing even harder beneath her fingers, Josie watched his head fall back.

"Fuck." The word escaped his lips, part whisper and part groan.

He'd always been in charge, she thought. In terms of experience, Carter was so far beyond her, it wasn't even funny. She was well out of her depth with him, but that didn't mean she had nothing to bring to the table. Swinging her legs over the edge of the bed, she rose to a sitting position. There were advantages to being the short girl, she thought as she leaned forward and took him in her mouth.

Carter closed his eyes at the sensation of her mouth on him. The soft press of her lips around his cock, the flick of her tongue against him...God above, it was amazing. It might actually kill him.

Sliding his hand into the thick fall of her hair, he gripped it tightly. Not so much to guide her, but because he needed something to hold on to. Every lick, every brush of her lips on his cock was like a little bit of heaven. With her hand moving over him, stroking him with a slow easy rhythm, her mouth working him in time, he knew he had to stop her. If he didn't, the night would be over before it even began.

"Josie," he groaned. "Baby, you have to stop."

"Let me," she urged. "I want to do this."

It took all of his strength to say no to that. It wasn't just a point of pride to make her come first. He *needed* to see her wild beneath him, to hear her moaning his name. The *why* was a little trickier, unless he wanted to analyze all the feelings he'd been trying so hard to avoid for so long. So instead, Carter just stepped back from her, easing her hands and her beautiful mouth off him.

"One day soon," he promised. "But not tonight. I know it's only been days, Josie, but that's just too goddamn long."

Moving onto the bed beside her, he pulled her with him so that she was sprawled across his lap, her legs straddling his hips, and her breasts pressed against his chest. Face-to-face, there was no mistaking the desire written plainly in her expression. He could feel the damp heat of her against him.

Carter parted the slick folds and eased inside her. Watching her face, seeing the pleasure reflected in her eyes, he lost himself in the power of that. He did that to her. Whatever else passed between them, no one else would ever make her feel the way he did.

The way her body closed around him, gripping him tightly, pulling him even deeper, had him struggling for control. Closing his arms around her, holding on to her tightly, he began to thrust into her, quick, shallow strokes that only fanned the flames and made them both burn hotter. It wasn't enough.

Carter slid his hands down her sides. Grasping her hips, he guided her movements, increasing the tempo and the force. Josie added a few moves of her own, clenching her muscles tightly around him, circling her hips in a way that practically made his eyes cross.

Her head was thrown back, her long hair brushing his thighs as she rode him. Dipping his head, he kissed her breasts, laving them with his tongue. Taking one taut peak into his mouth, he flicked his tongue over the hardened bud until Josie screamed for him. That was what he wanted. To drive her wild, to make her forget that she was supposed to be the good girl, the preacher's kid, the shining example that every other girl in town was meant to live up to. In that moment, he wanted her to be free of everything and just give in to her own feelings.

She clutched at him, her nails digging into his skin, her body taut and quivering against him. It was all heat and need driving them toward release. When she stiffened in his arms, every muscle clenching tightly, her inner muscles spasming rhythmically around him, Carter was lost. Sitting there on the edge of the bed, her legs and arms wrapped around him, her head on his shoulder, and both of them still trembling, he accepted the inevitable fact that she had the power to break him.

Somehow, without even trying to or possibly even wanting to, she'd burrowed so deep in him that he was never going to be free of her.

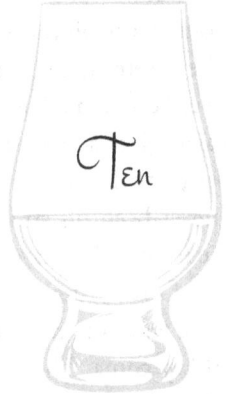

Ten

Carter waited at the end of the street for Josie. Thank the Lord it was cold out, and there were no kids out playing. As much time as he spent parked at the playground, he'd wind up on a registry somewhere.

She approached his truck and climbed in. "Was it awful?"

Her question was referencing the first-ever joint Darcy-Hayes Thanksgiving dinner. And it had been an utter disaster.

"Before or after Quentin Darcy and his newly discovered half brother got into a brawl on the front lawn?"

Her mouth dropped open. "You're kidding, right?"

"No, I'm not. But let's get the hell out of here before one of your nosy-ass neighbors makes all our sneaking pointless."

"Okay," she agreed. "I'm curious about this surprise you have for me."

He grinned. He'd been planning it for days. There was a special place on the farm where he'd always gone when he was a kid. It was his thinking spot, and he'd never shared it with anyone, but he wanted to take her there. He refused to think about the significance of that. Josie was still insisting that they were in the throes of some hot, steamy affair that would eventually just run its course. He had a suspicion it was a hell of a lot more than that.

Carter knew better than to push. She'd panic and bolt. Patience had never been his strong suit, but under the circumstances, he really didn't have any other choice.

They coasted out of town, rumbling past houses in his beat-up truck. No one was out and about. Everyone else was at home in a turkey coma. They were the only ones foolish enough not to be nursing full bellies with a ball game on television.

Deciding to start the sad tale of the first and probably last jointly celebrated holiday between the Darcy and Hayes families, he said, "Turns out Samuel has been a cheating bastard for a very long time."

"Not surprised," she replied. "You know about him and Erica McCoy?"

Everybody knew about him and Erica McCoy. "Oh, yeah. But this goes way back...There's another Darcy in town. A half sibling from Ireland."

He watched her eyes light up. For someone who never wanted to be the source of gossip, she sure ate it up.

"Really? He was there? What happened? Oh, dear heavens, what did Quentin Darcy do? Mia and Clayton, I imagine, would be at least cordial, but Quentin has an awful temper," she said.

She had it right. "Well, Quentin and the new guy wound up duking it out in the yard. I'll give the Celt his props. He handed Quentin his ass. It was a beautiful thing to see."

He hated Quentin Darcy. Well, he hated every Darcy,

in point of fact. He'd admit that Mia was growing on him just a little bit, but only to himself. If anyone ever asked him, he'd deny it with his last breath. Clayton, well, he was such a stand-up guy that he had to be tolerated at the very least. But Quentin was a fucking pig. Loud, brash, rude, a total asshole to everyone, and just generally a douchebag, they'd butted heads on more than one occasion over the years.

"So what did they fight about?" she asked.

Carter laughed. "They just don't much care for one another. Men fight because they like to fight, Josie. Hell, I'd punch Quentin Darcy for looking at me cross-eyed or walking down the wrong side of the street."

"So no one actually did anything? They just took an instant dislike to one another and started beating the hell out of each other?" she asked. "Poor Mia."

He'd missed something there. "What the hell does that mean, *poor Mia*?"

Josie rolled her eyes. "Do you have any idea how much work goes into putting on a Thanksgiving dinner for that many people? The cooking and planning and cleaning? She's worked on this for days and days, Carter. And because they had to behave like children, they spoiled all of her hard work. And the lot of you sat there laughing about it while she watched one of the first milestones of her and Bennett's relationship—a family holiday—go up in smoke."

"Well, of course I don't know how much work it is. I just show up and eat," he said. But now he was starting to feel bad for Mia, and that irked the hell out of him. Deciding to change the subject slightly, he added, "And the new Darcy is dating Loralei Crawford."

The distraction worked. Josie squealed. "Oh, that's fantastic. I love her to pieces. She was always so nice to me.

And her shop in Lexington is amazing. I'm too poor for just about everything in it, but she has the most beautiful things."

Carter made a mental note about that. He wasn't a total moron. "She looked good. Happy."

"So maybe the guy's not a total asshole."

He was a cocky son of a bitch, but probably not a total ass. Of course, Carter was also still giving him brownie points for breaking Quentin's perfect nose.

Turning the truck onto the gravel road, Carter hopped out and opened the gate. After driving through, he got out again and relocked it. It wasn't really a road, but there was a small rutted lane that cut down by the pastures, and he took it toward the woods that ran along the back half of the property. Parking at the edge of the trees, he walked around and opened her door for her. Those were the things he'd always been taught to do, and it bothered him more than a little that they were never in a situation where he was allowed to be a gentleman with her.

"Where exactly are you taking me, Carter?" she asked, looking at the tall trees with more than a little skepticism.

"You'll like it. I promise," he said, and grabbed the bag from the back. "It's not far from here."

Josie climbed out of the truck, her heels sinking into the gravel. He chuckled and, without hesitation, handed her the bag and then turned around. "How long's it been since you had a piggyback ride?"

"I am not doing that," she said.

"It's either that or let the gravel tear up those shoes... and I know how you feel about shoes." He grinned at her, knowing it would piss her off.

She sighed and then stepped back up on the truck's running board. Locking her arms around his neck and her legs around his waist, he hooked his arms beneath her knees for a little extra support. It shouldn't have been sexy, but it was Josie, and it involved her having her hands on him, and that was all it took.

Carter took the graveled path into the woods, where it eventually gave way to just dirt and finally opened up into the clearing where he'd played as a boy. The creek ran close by and could be heard through the trees. Piles of leaves covered the hard-packed earth, but in the center was the surprise.

He'd made a bed of old pallets and suspended it from the surrounding trees. With a foam mattress and a few blankets and pillows, it was a quiet retreat for them. He'd strung lanterns in the trees, as well. He'd swiped the ideas from Savannah's sketch book and had to admit that it was definitely worth the effort.

"Carter, this is beautiful."

He looked around, trying to see it through her eyes. The ancient oak trees were so tall they seemed to stretch all the way to heaven. The rustling leaves beneath their feet and the soft, soothing sound of flowing water made it just about perfect in his mind.

"I thought you'd like it out here," he said. "I used to come here when I was little. I stayed at the farm a lot with Mamaw and Papaw. After he died, Mamaw let Emmitt have the farm, and she bought that little house in town where Bennett lives now."

"Did you want the farm?" she asked him.

He laughed. "Oh, hell no. I hate farming. I'll help Emmitt when I have to, but I'd rather take a beating. No, I got what I wanted. Papaw left me his truck, and I'll drive it till it won't go another foot."

Josie just looked at him for the longest time. This sentimental side of him wasn't something she'd expected from him. Grand romantic gestures like building them a bed in the trees? Well, she hadn't expected that either.

"You really loved him, didn't you?"

Carter smiled. "He never told me I was like my dad. He never compared me to anybody else or looked at me like he was just waiting for me to get in trouble. And I spent more time with him than just about anybody. Mama worked so much. It was hard for her, which I understand now, but when you're a kid, things like money and having to work just don't make a whole lot of sense."

Josie smiled as she climbed up on the edge of the suspended bed and then scooted back to lie down and look up at the sky through the barren trees. It would be dark soon, and as clear as it was, they'd see the stars like pinholes in the sky.

"It doesn't make much sense now, honestly. I question every day why I was so determined to work at the library...and why, as awful as Doris is, I don't just give up. She'll never give me a moment's peace as long as I'm there."

Carter gave the bed a push. It was suspended with springs that allowed it to swing.

Josie closed her eyes and let the rocking motion take her away from everything. "I can't believe you did this for me," she said.

"There's not a lot I wouldn't do for you," he answered easily. "And while I mean that in every perverted way you can imagine, I mean it in others too."

She opened her eyes and looked at him then. He was

smiling, but there was something different in his eyes that she hadn't seen before.

"Are you going to stand there all evening, or are you going to join me?" she asked.

Carter obliged, climbing onto the bed with her. It swayed with their combined weight, rocking back and forth. He pulled her close, and she just let herself melt against him. Lying there surrounded by nature, her head on his chest and his arms around her, Josie beat down the panic, the fear that something so good couldn't possibly last. Instead, she just snuggled against him and vowed to savor it while she could.

"Do you think Bennett and Mia will get married?" she asked.

He chuckled. "Should I be worried about how interested you are in them?"

She rose onto her elbow and looked at him. "Mia and Bennett are like Romeo and Juliet, Carter. Everyone in town is that interested in them. I just have an inside track for intel. Will they?"

"Eventually. Ten years is a long time to be apart, even when you do love someone. Maybe *especially* when you love someone," he answered. "They need to get comfortable with one another again, and they need to figure out how to be together without having to sneak around."

There was a note in his tone, an implication that maybe they needed to work on that too. Josie sighed and let her head drop onto his chest again.

"I'm just as bad as everyone else in this town. Poking my nose into people's business, asking questions about things that don't concern me at all."

"There's a difference," he said.

"How's that?" she asked.

Carter dropped one leg over the side of the swing,

pushing off again so it kept rocking gently. "Because you care. You're not asking because you want to see them fail. You're asking because you want to see them succeed. You might be stubborn and ornery, you might have a temper like a wildcat, but you're a good person, Josephine Marcum. Not just surface good, but deep down where it counts."

Josie closed her eyes, willing herself not to cry. She was all the things he'd said, every last one of them, and more. But he still believed that she was good. With Carter, she was always *enough*.

If they went public and told people they were together, how many of those people who'd reminded her all her life that she had so much to be grateful for would do the same thing again? All of them. They'd talk about how handsome he was, how tall he was, and then they'd hint that maybe her children wouldn't be midgets. Or, heaven forbid, they failed epically in front of everyone. Then she'd hear about how lucky she was to have dodged the bullet of being tied to a man like him.

"Do you ever just want to run away from here and go some place where no one knows a thing about you?" she asked.

He pushed the swing off again, pulled her tighter. "Every damn day."

"Can we stay out here all night?" she asked. "Or are you working tomorrow?"

"No. I told Savannah I'd never work another Black Friday as long as I live. It's going to get cold," he warned.

"We have blankets...and body heat." She waggled her eyebrows as she said it.

He laughed. "Don't ever do that again. Please. I can't unsee that."

"It's not sexy?" she asked, climbing on top of him.

Straddling his hips, her hands flat on his chest, she looked down at him. "Would it be sexier if I did it sitting right here?"

He didn't say anything, just settled his hands on her hips, tugging their bodies closer together, grinding against her. "You can do anything you want as long as you do it sitting right there."

Josie unzipped her jacket and tossed it to the side. The air was cool, but still mild enough. Thankfully, all the rain had finally cleared. She hadn't really dressed for seduction. Jeans, high-heeled boots, and a twin set didn't exactly scream sex kitten. With that thought in mind, she reached for the hem of her sweater, but he stopped her, his hands closing around her wrists.

"Unbutton it...slowly. One at a time."

Josie smiled. "Any other requests?"

"That'll do to start," he answered.

Josie reached for the bottom button, working it free slowly. His hands stroked her back, her hips, her ass. He touched her everywhere except the places she needed to be touched most, but he didn't want to hurry, and for a change, neither did she. Carter had built them an oasis there in the woods, and it was magic. No need to rush or hurry, no need to hide or sneak or pretend.

With the last button freed, she slipped the sweater off her shoulders and let it fall to the bed. His hands moved from her hips to her waist, his thumbs sliding beneath the hem of the camisole she'd worn underneath. Josie pulled the camisole over her head. The contrast of cool air and his hot hands on her skin made her shiver.

"Too cold?" he asked.

"No...you make me shiver for a completely different reason," she answered honestly.

He grinned at her then, the same sexy smirk that

always made her either want to kiss him or choke him. It was definitely the former that was on her mind. Leaning forward, resting her weight on her palms, she pressed her lips to his. She kissed him slowly, molding her lips to his, savoring the sensation of his beard against her skin, the slight clenching of his fingers on her thighs.

Josie licked his bottom lip, her tongue gliding over the curve of his mouth. But Carter would never be a passive participant. She was on top, but when he kissed her back, his mouth hot and hungry on hers, there was no denying that he was in control. Her body melted against him, her breasts crushed against his chest, the hard ridge of his erection nestled at the apex of her thighs. She wanted more. She wanted to be naked against him, to feel him moving inside her, easing the ache that he created.

Breaking the kiss, she drew back. "I need to get these boots off so I can get these damned pants off. Remind me to only wear skirts with you from now on."

Carter simply pushed her off him and onto the bed, still on her stomach. "Lift your hips."

She did, and he reached beneath her to unfasten her jeans. Within seconds, he had them yanked down to her knees. She felt him behind her, heard the rasp of his zipper, and then simply dropped her head to the mattress and moaned as he pushed into her.

It was like that every time. Right. Perfect. Her mood didn't matter, whether she wanted him to be tender or rough. He just seemed to know without question what she needed from him. And at that moment, he was moving achingly slow, sinking into her inch by inch, filling her up until she could do nothing but grip the bedding and sob his name.

"Josie, let go, baby," he whispered, his hands stroking

over her back, her hips. He was so tender and so gentle with her. "Let go."

With his hands holding her hips steady, he set a slow but devastating rhythm—hard thrusts followed by an agonizingly slow retreat that only dragged out the pleasure. Josie couldn't think, couldn't focus. Hell, she could barely *breathe*. It was as if the entirety of her existence had narrowed to just the two of them.

His hands moved from her hips, coasting up her back, to her shoulders, and then down her arms. His hands covered hers, his breath hot against her neck as he kissed the tender spot where her neck and shoulder met. When his teeth closed there, biting down just hard enough, she was simply lost. Her hips bucked beneath him. Her eyes closed, and she literally saw stars as the pleasure exploded inside her, wave after wave of it. He pumped his hips again, twice more, and then he stilled as well.

The weight of him was heavy on her, solid. But it felt good. It made her feel safe and protected, secure in a way that she rarely did.

She was in love with him.

It should have made her panic. It should have sent her running. But lying there beneath him, listening to the sound of his breathing, feeling the soft stroke of his hand on her skin, she willed the fear away. It would come back later, and it would be ugly. But for now, she just wanted to enjoy the feeling of being in his arms in the small, perfect space he'd made for them.

Eleven

J osie left the last store with another bag weighing her down. The annual Black Friday Christmas shopping with her mom was fun normally, but today she was tired and cranky. And depressed. She admitted it. Realizing that she was in love with Carter should have been a happy moment, an exciting one. But it just left her petrified.

What if he didn't love her back? What if he couldn't?

"You know, Josie, Myra Simmons's nephew was very taken with you at church last week."

Myra Simmons's nephew made her skin crawl. "Mom, I do not need you to play matchmaker."

Deborah stopped walking and placed her hand on Josie's arm. It was her mom face, her I'm-worried-but-you-can-still-decide-for-yourself face.

"He's a more suitable young man for you, Josie. I know you don't want to be alone."

She didn't want to be alone. But she didn't want to be with just anyone, either. She only wanted Carter.

"I can't. I just...I'm not interested in him that way."

"Josie, you barely know him. You just need to give him a chance. You know he's going to seminary. He's going to be a minister."

And there it was. The real reason for the push.

"Mom, I know you love being a preacher's wife. You love being active in the church and taking care of the congregation...I don't. I don't want to do those things. I want to work around books, and I want to go home at night and read more books. And I don't want to feel responsible for everybody."

Deborah started walking away, but Josie knew the conversation wasn't over. When her mother got something in her head like that, she was a pit bull.

"It can be a very rewarding life, Josephine. It gives you strength and courage."

"It gives *you* strength and courage. You. Not me. I just want books," Josie insisted.

Deborah nodded. "You're sure you won't even have lunch with him?"

"Yes. I'm sure."

Deborah clucked her tongue. "Myra will be so disappointed. She really wanted to see you all get together."

Not likely, Josie thought. Myra was just angling for a better social position within the church. Not that Myra was a bad person. She wasn't. She was actually a very good person, but there was definitely a hierarchy at play among the female portion of the congregation.

"She'll adjust," Josie said conversationally. "Mom, would you—Never mind."

"What is it, Josie?"

"I have to tell you the truth. I've been seeing Carter."

Deborah nodded. "I know that. I know you, and I could tell that something was different for you. Are you in love with him?"

Two middle-aged men vacated one of the benches outside the department store, and Josie made a beeline for it. She sat down and tucked the bags beneath her. If they were going to talk about Carter, it was best to do it there rather than anywhere in Fontaine, where every set of ears in town would be pressed against the door.

"I don't really know. I think so. But I've never been in love. I've never even thought that I was in love," she admitted. "Is there something wrong with me?"

Deborah smiled sadly. "Josie, you were a year old when we brought you home. And you hated to be held. You hated for us to touch you. You'd cry because you were hungry or dirty, then you'd cry because we were feeding you or changing you. I felt like the worst failure as a mother. I thought, in those moments when you were screaming like we were killing you, that maybe God had been right not to give me any babies. Clearly, I had no skill at soothing one."

"I'm sorry I was so awful," Josie whispered, feeling even more guilty than ever.

Deborah looked at her then with tears in her eyes. "But you weren't, my sweet girl. You were only scared. No one had held you before. When you'd been fed and changed before, it had been rough or perfunctory at best. You were afraid because you'd never known what it was like to have someone touch you with actual tenderness... with love. So you cried every time, until one day, maybe a month or so later, you just didn't. I was holding you and rocking you and you just let me. You stared up at me with those big gray eyes, like you'd finally put two and two together, and knew that we wouldn't hurt you."

Josie couldn't speak for the lump in her throat. She clenched her hands together in her lap and just stared at the ground. She couldn't imagine what it must have been like, the patience and the faith that it had taken for her mother to keep trying day in and day out.

"Everyone always told me how lucky I was, and I know they're right." She finally managed. "But I didn't know how right."

Deborah sighed. "And it stroked my ego, Josie. I try to be the best Christian I can be, but I have pride just like everyone else. And when people would say that to you, I should have stopped them right there and said that *we* were the lucky ones. But I didn't. Because they always talked about our faith, being good Christians, about doing the Lord's work. And at first, I felt like letting them have that little bit of sympathy for where you'd come from. I didn't think it hurt anything. But I was wrong. It hurt you. Every time. And I was too blinded by my own piety to see it."

"Why are you telling me all this now?"

Deborah squared her shoulders. "Because part of you is still that scared baby who doesn't trust anyone that touches her gently. Is he good to you?"

"Carter is wonderful to me," she said. "He really isn't what people say he is, Mom. I'm not in any way suggesting that he's an angel, or that he hasn't sown more than his share of wild oats, but that's not all there is to him."

"Then invite him to church. If you want this thing between you all to last, you can't just keep sneaking around forever. It might be fun. It might feel decadent and forbidden, but that wears off after a while, Josephine. Bring him to church and go from there."

Josie tried to imagine how that invitation would go over. Not well. Not well at all. But she'd try. She had no other choice.

Twelve

Carter's muscles strained as he hoisted his end of the heavy cabinet onto the bed of the truck. Christ, he was tired. He'd lost count of how many pieces of heavy-ass furniture he'd moved that day. At the rate they were going, they'd be out of stock before Christmas. Which meant more auctions, estate sales, and stripping houses before demolitions. And all of that meant more time out of town and away from Josie.

Hell, maybe that was a good thing. They were into the first week of December. The idyllic Thanksgiving afternoon seemed like it was a million years ago. Both of them had been too busy or too tired to carve out a minute for one another since then. Sure, they'd texted and called, but it wasn't the same as seeing her, holding her. But even that was growing frustrating.

A few stolen hours weren't cutting it anymore. He wanted to hold her through the night and wake up with her the next morning. He wanted lazy Saturday mornings in bed. Those were things that, if he was totally honest with himself, he'd never really wanted before. And he didn't believe for a second that she was actually ready to give that to him.

The cabinet slipped, mostly because he was distracted, and he banged his knuckles on the tailgate. Biting back a vicious curse, he wrestled the damn thing into the bed and then headed back inside, leaving Bennett to secure it.

Heading for the workroom, he rinsed his bloodied knuckles in the sink there. Most of it was minor scrapes, but a good chunk was missing from one knuckle in partic-ular. Getting sawdust in that would burn like a mother. Digging through the cabinet, Carter found the first aid kit that they rarely used and even more rarely kept stocked. Hopefully, there'd be a few stray Band-Aids.

The door opened, and he cursed, thinking it would be Bennett bitching at him for leaving him to deal with the cabinet. "I'm not in the damn mood, Bennett."

"Not in the mood for what, exactly?"

That wasn't Bennett. Shit. Shit. Shit. The day just kept getting better, he thought.

Turning around, Carter found himself face-to-face with William Marcum.

"I'm sorry for cussing. I thought you were someone else."

William gestured to Carter's bloody hand. "Looks like you've got a reason to. I'm assuming you busted that moving furniture and not smashing your cousin's face in?"

"It was a cabinet, actually," Carter replied. Moving away from the sink, he leaned against one of the workta-bles. It wasn't a social call. He knew that.

"So what can I do for you?"

William didn't pretty it up with niceties. "You can tell me what your intentions are for my daughter."

Carter nodded thoughtfully. "That's easier said than

done...and it needs to be said between Josie and me. Not you. But I will tell you one thing...I don't want to hurt her, ever. Whatever happens, I want to see Josie happy."

"Are you in love with my daughter?" William demanded.

"If I am, I probably ought to tell her before I tell you," Carter said. "I get that you're concerned, and I don't blame you for it. But Josie is an adult, and she's entitled to make her own choices. For the moment, I'm one of them."

William put his hands in his pockets and rocked back on his heels. "For the moment? So you don't see this as permanent."

He wanted that. The realization that he wanted her forever cut him deep. Mostly because he knew she probably didn't feel the same. Even if she did, she'd be too terrified to reach out and grab onto what she wanted because people might think badly of her and the man in front of him. Since Josie wasn't there to take the brunt of his anger, he unleashed it on William instead.

"Even if I did, I couldn't have it. This town has made up their mind about me. They, and you, think they know all there is to know about me. And Josie's so damn terrified to disappoint you that she'll never publicly do anything that goes against her good girl image."

William shook his head. "That's an excuse, son."

"No, it isn't," Carter countered. "It's reality. You don't know. You have no idea just how broken she is. You've been so busy getting pats on the back for adopting the little orphan girl that you never even stopped to look at what it was doing to her every time someone said it!"

The anger and frustration were boiling inside him, and Carter just let it go. "Yes, I drink. But I'm not a drunk. Yes, I like women, but I didn't sleep with every one that crossed my path. I don't lie, and I sure as hell don't go out of my way to hurt other people...but to every judgmental person in this whole damn town, I'll never be anything but the bastard son of James Carter, a drunk, a cheat, and a reckless dumbass who turned his back on the wrong man in a bar."

"Son, you can be anything you want to be," William said.

Carter turned away and placed his palms flat on the table. It was either that or punch something. "I already *am* exactly what I want to be. But no one sees it, and I'm tired as hell of trying to make them. You want to know what's going to happen between me and Josie? I suggest you ask her. She's been the one calling the shots from the get-go."

William started to walk away, but at the door to the workroom, he paused. "Maybe people in this town don't see who you really are...and I know they gossip, and I know they judge. But this is a good place. People help each other here. They care about what happens to one another. And in all fairness, you've only ever shown them the aspects of you that would remind them of your father. If there is something different from that inside of you, Carter, maybe you need to let it shine for a change."

Carter didn't say anything else, just listened to the sound of the door closing. He needed to see Josie, and he needed to see her where they wouldn't actually do anything other than talk. Whether she liked it or not.

Josie gave a sigh of relief as Doris left the library. It was her weekly lunch with her sister, where they'd sit in Gruber's

Diner and plot all the ways to get Josie fired so they could hire Doris's niece. Let them plot. It gave her a moment's peace from Doris's critical eye and constant hounding.

Standing behind the circulation desk, she looked up when the door opened, half afraid that Doris had come back. But it wasn't Doris. Jordan Simmons was walking in, Myra's nephew, who wanted to take her out. *No. No. No. No. No.*

She'd told her mother to nip that in the bud, and she'd really thought that maybe they'd reached an understanding that day. Maybe not, she thought.

"Good afternoon, Josie," he said, smiling. It wasn't a bad smile. He wasn't a bad-looking man. But he left her completely cold.

"Good afternoon, Jordan. Is there something I can help you with?" *Keep it professional, and get him gone*, she thought.

His smile widened. "My aunt and your mother have been trying to do a little matchmaking...or didn't you know about that?"

No keeping it professional. She'd give him points for at least getting to the point. "I was aware of that, Jordan, but I'm sorry. That's just not something I really want to pursue right now."

"Josie, I know we haven't spent a lot of time together, but I have a tremendous amount of respect for you. You've accomplished so much."

No, she hadn't. She was a passable piano player because she'd been forced to practice until she just wanted to vomit. She'd gotten a college degree and had graduated with a decent GPA, mostly because it was a subject that she loved and came easy to her. Nothing about that was grand or especially noteworthy. Unless he was implying something else, and if he was, it was going to get ugly.

"Given the very rough start you had in life, it's really amazing to see just how far you've come."

He was going there, Josie realized. He was actually going there.

"Jordan, I don't think—"

"Josie, I have every intention of completing seminary by the end of next year, and I'm not looking to date women who don't understand what it means to be a godly wife."

And he clearly didn't intend to date women who ever wanted to speak because he didn't intend to shut up.

"I'd really like to see if we're compatible, Josie. I'd like to take you to dinner this weekend so we can start to get to know one another."

Start to get to know one another. He had yet to even ask if she wanted to get to know him.

"I am very flattered by your offer, Jordan, but I explained this to my mother, and she should have passed it along to Myra. I have no interest in being a minister's wife. I do know exactly how much work goes into that and how hard it can be to meet those standards. I don't want that kind of life, Jordan."

His smile never wavered. "You're very young, Josie, and I know that temptation can be so strong, but if you pray about it, and ask for God to speak to you and show you the way—"

"I don't need God to show me the way on this one," she said sharply. "I don't want to date you. The truth is, I'm already seeing someone."

She didn't know who was more stunned by the admission, her or Jordan. It hadn't been her intention to say anything about Carter. But it felt good.

His smile wavered. For the first time since he walked in the building, Jordan Simmons looked like maybe he wasn't going to make the sale. "I didn't realize. You've never brought him to church with you."

There was an accusation buried in that. But Josie elected to ignore it. "He doesn't attend church."

Jordan drew back like she'd told him she was contagious. "I heard the rumors, but I dismissed them. You can't possibly be seeing Carter Hayes."

"It's none of your business who I'm seeing, Jordan," she said pointedly. His tone, his posture, and the dismissive way he'd said Carter's name, as if he were a nonperson, just rubbed her the wrong way. "I think you should go. This conversation is over."

Jordan's entire demeanor changed. His face softened, his expression taking on a hint of contrition and even tenderness, which was just bizarre.

When he grabbed her hand, holding it so tightly she couldn't pull away without hurting herself, he said, "Josie, I didn't mean to hurt your feelings. Let me make it up to you. At the very least, I can take you to lunch."

She shook her head. "That isn't necessary. Please let me go."

He lifted her hand to his lips and kissed it, an old-fashioned and, coming from him, frankly, creepy gesture that made her skin crawl. "I'll see you Sunday," he said.

Josie watched him turn and walk away, wondering what the hell that had been about. But when she turned, she realized exactly what he'd been doing. Carter had come in through the library's side entrance and was standing just far enough away to have only seen their exchange and not heard it.

Walking toward him, Josie could see the banked fury in his expression.

"Carter, I don't know what you're thinking, but you're wrong," she said.

"No, I'm not. Isn't that the kind of guy you want, Josie? Someone who doesn't embarrass you? Who doesn't reflect poorly on your raising?" His voice was low, but there was no disguising just how mad he was.

"Jordan came here to ask me on a date, but I turned him down," she stated. "I don't want him."

Carter shook his head. "Wanting isn't enough, Josie."

He turned to leave, and Josie felt panic clawing at her. "Carter, don't walk out on me...not like this."

"Then walk out with me," he said. "Right now."

She couldn't. If she left the library, she'd lose her job. Giving up her independence and moving home with her parents wasn't an option. "I can't do that. Carter—"

"Forget it, Josie."

He left, the door slamming behind him, and it didn't feel like just for the moment. It was big and ugly and felt like a hard goodbye.

"I'm not ready," she said in a whisper. She wasn't ready to go completely public with their relationship, but she wasn't ready for it to end, either. "Dammit."

Thirteen

The truck's powerful engine rumbled as Clayton Darcy extricated himself from the back seat. He was drunk off his ass, and they'd probably all hear about it tomorrow from Mia and Annalee, Carter thought. If anyone had told him that he'd be out drinking with a Darcy, much less with the rest of the Hayes clan with him, he'd have called them a damn liar.

But his mind wasn't really on Clayton or even on the game they'd just watched while consuming excessive amounts of beer and more than their fair share of shots. It was *her*. She was in his fucking head, mixing it all up and making him crazy. It had been like that from day one, and he was tired of it. He knew he'd been an ass the other day at the library. He'd been jealous and mean, jumping to conclusions.

He'd walked out too, and that wasn't something she'd forgive easily. That was evidenced by the fact that she hadn't called him, texted, or tried to reach out to him in any way. They were both pouting like overgrown children.

He glanced over toward her house. It was one of the

smaller homes in the subdivision where Clayton Darcy lived. It had been hell sneaking around in that neighborhood and trying not to be seen, but again, that had been her choice. She was the one who wanted to hide, who wanted to pretend like they were nothing to each other.

The light was on upstairs in her bedroom. Was she in bed reading one of the smutty novels she liked? Or was she watching some sappy TV show while eating ice cream? He knew her habits. He knew so much about her, and yet in public, they'd never shared more than a few words.

Clayton stumbled up the driveway and managed to get himself into the house. Emmitt, the only one of them still sober, shifted the truck into drive. It surged forward but had gone no more than fifty feet before Carter yelled out. "Stop the truck!"

"You puke in here and I'm gonna kick your ass!" Emmitt shouted.

"Just let me out, dammit!" Carter replied.

Bennett shifted forward in his seat, and Carter moved past him through the open door. He crossed the road and marched toward her front door. He was done with hiding. She wanted him to be some big secret, something on the side while she played the good girl in front of the whole town. He was done with that shit.

Raising his fist, he pounded on the door. "Josie! I know you're in there!"

In the truck, Bennett looked at Emmitt. "Did you know about this?"

"Ain't that Josie Marcum's house?" Emmitt shot back. "What the hell would she be doing with Carter?"

Bennet raised his eyebrow. "What do all women do with Carter?"

"True enough...but Josie Marcum? Hell."

They watched him walk up to her door. Bennett asked, "Should we wait for him?"

"Hell, no!" Emmitt said. "I'm not sitting outside waiting for his ass while he gets laid!"

"We don't know that he's getting laid," Bennett protested.

Emmitt made a noise of complete derision. "It's Carter, and she's female. Hell, she'll probably greet him pussy first."

"Jesus, you're crude," Bennett said with a shake of his head.

"Yeah, well, I'm not in love, so I don't have to pretty it all up," Emmitt said and eased the truck into drive. "She can drive his ass home when she's done with him."

On the porch, Carter was preparing to bang on the door again when the porch light suddenly flicked on. The door opened a crack, and he could see Josie peering out at him.

"What are you doing here?" she hissed at him.

"Open the damn door, and let me in!" he barked.

"I will not!"

"If you don't," he replied, "I will stand out here making so damn much noise one of your uptight neighbors will call the cops. It'll be all over town by morning, Josie, that I got arrested on your doorstep!"

Her eyes widened. "You wouldn't dare."

Carter smiled, but it wasn't a friendly expression. There was none of his usual charm in it. Instead, it was mean and even a little vicious.

"You ought to know better than anybody that there's not a lot I won't do. Now open the damn door!"

The door closed, and he heard the lock click and the chain slide free. When she opened it and stepped back, he didn't hesitate, but just barged in, slamming the door behind him.

"What do you think you're doing?" she demanded. "Do you have any idea what people will say?"

"The truth?" he asked. "That I've been sneaking over here and fucking you for over a month? That I make you scream and beg and say the kind of words that would have everybody at the First Baptist Church praying for your soul?"

She rolled her eyes heavenward. "Just because I don't want to trot my business out for everyone in town *or* be lumped in with all the other women you string along—"

"String along?" he demanded. He was so angry he wanted to shake her. Instead, he ran his fingers through his hair in a gesture of frustration and annoyance. "Since I bumped into you in that damn bar in Cincinnati, I haven't had time for a conversation with another woman, much less the time to string one along! And if anyone's doing any stringing here, it's you!"

"Me? I don't think so, Carter Hayes. You're welcome to walk anytime you want to. In fact, you already did, without a backward glance! Find someone else to have your fun with!"

He laughed at that, but it was a humorless sound.

She continued, all but shouting. "That's all this has been for you, anyway. Just a little bit of fun, right? Isn't that what you said? We'd stop when it wasn't fun for either of us anymore."

"Oh, yeah. This is so much fun," he snarked. It was fun like ramming your face into a brick wall.

He started to walk out. Hell, he wasn't even sure why he came there. It had been a beer-fueled impulse, and now he wasn't sure if he regretted it or not. He glanced back at

115

her. She was clearly mad as hell. Her arms were crossed over her chest, and her chin was up. But it was the look of hurt and disappointment in her eyes that made him stop. He'd known she could hurt him. She had more times already than he could count. But he'd never thought, not even for a second, that he had the power to hurt her.

"Fuck it," he whispered and turned back to her.

He grasped her wrist, tugging her forward until she was pressed against him. She wore nothing or next to nothing beneath the robe she had on. His hands went to her hair immediately, tugging her head back until she was looking up at him. Her lips were parted, not in surprise, but in anticipation. Lowering his mouth to hers, he kissed her, his lips moving over hers with all the urgency that he felt. He didn't want to lose her, but he wasn't going to take the scraps either.

Sliding his tongue between her lips, the kiss took on a note that was blatantly carnal. He wasn't even sure how it happened, but suddenly her back was against the wall, and her legs were wrapped around his waist. His cock was so hard he thought it might literally kill him, and she was moaning into his mouth. Drawing back, Carter looked at her, at the flush in her cheeks and her kiss-swollen lips. Without a drop of makeup on her face, she was the most beautiful woman he'd ever laid eyes on. If he unzipped his pants, he could be inside her in less than ten seconds. And he was going to walk away.

"I'm not doing this with you anymore, Josie. You want to fuck me, then you're going to have to date me."

"Excuse me?" she said, blinking at him in confusion.

"You heard me," he said. "If you want me in your bed, then you're going to be seen with me...in public." He stepped back, and her legs unlocked from his waist until she was standing on her own two feet. "You know where to find me."

"That's it?" she asked, her brain still clearly muddled from the *slightly-more-than-just-a-kiss.* "You're leaving now?"

"I mean it, Josie. I want you. I want you so bad right now it's fucking killing me. But I'm not going to just be the man you're sleeping with."

"What are you going to be, then?"

"If you'd let me, I'd be the man who loves you."

She said nothing, but her eyes widened, and her jaw went slightly slack. He'd dropped a bomb on her, and he'd just leave it to sink in.

Carter opened the door and walked out into the night. Bennett and Emmitt were long gone. It wouldn't be the first time he'd walked home, probably wouldn't be the last, because he didn't believe for a second that Josie Marcum would ditch her good girl image to slum it with him.

But there was a little spark of hope. It was enough to keep him going.

Josie watched him walk away. She didn't try to stop him, not because she didn't want to, but because her body had simply stopped responding to her brain. Stunned, more than a little drunk on the bottle of wine she'd consumed not long before Carter banged on her door, she couldn't think or function.

There was still some wine left, and she needed it. Forcing her feet to move, one in front of the other, she entered the kitchen and grabbed the bottle from the counter. She didn't even bother with a glass, but just drained it completely as she walked back to the living room and flopped down on the couch, the empty bottle rolling from her hand.

"He didn't actually say he loved me," she told herself. "Just that he wanted to."

Oh, she needed to talk to her mother. But calling her up this late at night, half drunk, and after having Carter banging on the door loud enough for all the neighbors to hear? Actually, her mother was probably already up because one of those neighbors would have called her.

Even as the thought crossed her mind, her cell phone buzzed on the table. Josie fumbled for it, finally managed to close her hand around it, and accepted the call.

"Hey, Mom." The words were slurred, but not horribly.

"Did that boy get you drunk, Josephine?"

"No," Josie admitted. "I got myself drunk long before he showed up. He says he wants to date me. Publicly. That he's tired of sneaking around. He said—" She stopped there. Even drunk, she wasn't sure she could say that to her mother.

"Josephine, just tell me. Dear heavens!"

Josie lay back down on the couch and looked up at the ceiling. It wasn't spinning, but it was a little wobbly.

"He said that he doesn't want to be just the man I'm sleeping with...that he wants to be the man who loves me, if I'll let him."

Deborah went silent for a minute, thinking before speaking. "Then you should invite him to church."

It was such a typical answer from her mother that Josie could only laugh. "He'll say no."

"No, he won't. If he wants your relationship to be

public, then there is no better way to say that 'I am serious about this girl' than to attend church with her. Ask him and see."

The wine hit her hard, and all she wanted was sleep.

"Tomorrow," Josie said. "I'm going to talk to him tomorrow."

Fourteen

Carter was hungover as hell. Rolling onto his back, he stared up at the ceiling and willed himself not to puke. After leaving Josie's house, *after making an ass of himself,* he thought, he'd come home and finished off a bottle of Fire Creek that had been in the cabinet. It had been a horrible, awful, stupid mistake.

Gingerly, he sat up, put his feet on the floor, and focused all his energy on not tossing his proverbial cookies. She was making him crazy. He was so turned inside out by her that he literally didn't know if he was coming or going, and he didn't even know how the hell it had happened.

Forcing himself to get to his feet, Carter walked from the bedroom to the bathroom under his own steam. He was buck naked and smelled like a barroom.

Shower, he thought. He needed a shower. He needed to never smell bourbon again. Or for someone to just kill him and end his misery. That would work. He could call Emmitt. Emmitt would happily end his life since his stunt with the library book on erectile dysfunction had apparently blown the gossip mill wide open. Emmitt was less than pleased with him, to put it mildly.

Turning on the taps, he waited for the water to warm and leaned his aching head against the cool tile. He pressed his whole face against it and let out a groan at the relief it provided.

The pounding on the door only echoed the pounding in his head. "Fuck. Just fuck."

Turning the taps back off, he cursed again. It would take a million years to get the water hot at this rate. Whoever was at his door, he intended to make them go away quick. He was in no mood. Rather than get dressed, he just grabbed a towel from the shelf and wrapped it around his waist as he half stumbled to the door.

Yanking it open, he found himself face-to-face with the woman who was responsible for his misery. Josie stood there, looking almost as miserable as he felt. There was just enough meanness in him to appreciate that. He let his eyes wander, taking her in from head to toe. She was wearing a sweater dress and a pair of the high-heeled boots she favored, but there were dark circles under her eyes, and she looked more than a little green around the gills.

"You look awful," she said.

"You don't look much better." The retort was snappy, his tone clipped. He didn't know what the hell she was doing there, but it probably wasn't good.

"Let me in, Carter," she said, clearly in no mood to tolerate his shit.

"Afraid somebody will see you out there?"

"No. But I am afraid of freezing my tail off. Stop being an asshole!"

He shrugged and stepped back, leaving the door open for her to come inside. He was being a dick, and it was only partially because of the hangover. Crying over her wasn't an option, so that left being a first-class prick.

"What do you want, Josephine?"

"To talk. There are a few things we need to clear up," she said softly.

"Like what?"

"Jordan Simmons."

Just the name made him want to punch something. He didn't believe for a second that Josie had any interest in that pompous little shit. It had been a knee-jerk reaction when he'd first seen them together. Jealousy was an ugly feeling, and one he wasn't accustomed to. But later on, when he'd been thinking more clearly, it had bothered him for other reasons.

If Josie walked down Main Street with Simmons, people would smile and nod, perfectly pleased with the pairing of the current minister's daughter and the minister in training. It didn't matter that Simmons was a first-class asshole and a sneaky piece of shit. He played the game, he looked the part, and everyone in town bowed and scraped to him. Meanwhile, they looked at him like he was something dirty they'd stepped in.

"I don't have fuck-all to say about Jordan Simmons. He's a smarmy shit, and we both know it."

She raised her eyebrows at that. "Funny, you seemed to have a very different take on things the other day."

"I flew off the handle a little. That's what I do."

"No, it isn't. You don't have some wild temper. You don't yell or scream or get mad...except with me. I make you crazy," she said. "Because I'm a giant pain in the ass."

He didn't disagree with her. Every bit of that was true. She was also sweet, and so damn pretty it hurt to look at her sometimes, and funny, and unfailingly kind. And her being a pain in the ass wasn't always a flaw. At times, it was one of the things he liked best about her. His cupcake didn't take any shit.

"You do make me crazy," he said. "In a lot of ways."

She moved deeper into the room and perched on the arm of the couch. "You're right to be mad at me, to tell me to stop being so scared of other people's opinions. The only opinion that ought to matter to me is yours."

That brought him up short. Standing there in nothing but a towel and reeking of bourbon and heaven only knew what else, he just couldn't make sense of it.

"Why would my opinion be the only one that matters?"

"Did you mean what you said last night? That you wanted to be the man who loved me?"

Fuck, he had not meant to say that. Being pissed and drunk made him too damned honest for his own good. But there was no taking it back.

"Hell, Josie...I *am* the man who loves you. Do you honestly think I'd have snuck around and carried on the way I did with you for any other reason? If all I wanted was to get laid, I could have done that without working nearly as hard."

"Well, that's pretty."

He chuckled a little. In spite of his shitty mood, his aching head, and the fact that his guts clearly no longer wanted to stay on the inside, her caustic tone still managed to tickle him.

"It's the truth. There are a lot of women in this town who would have been more than happy to parade around with me...at least for the short term. That's what I am to most of them. Short term. The guy you have fun with before you go and find one to settle down with who has a good job, and a solid future, and a stable income."

"You have all those things. I know how hard you work

to help Savannah with Revision," she protested. "You're not just an employee there, Carter. You're a partner."

"People don't see me that way. They don't want to. They've got ideas about who I am, and they're comfortable with 'em. Same way with you. People wouldn't bat an eye if you walked out with Simmons because, to their mind, you all belong together. The one place you don't belong would be with me." It hurt to admit that. It stung like a hundred slivers of glass slicing into him at once.

"They're wrong," she said softly. "I'm a hypocrite, Carter. I curse. I drink. I have hot, steamy affairs with the town bad boy. And I do it all while looking down my nose at people who look down their nose at me. I'm not perfect. I'm not even good most of the time. I just hide all the wickedness so no one sees."

"That isn't true. Well...not all of that is true."

Josie shrugged. "Close enough to the truth. But I don't want to be that person. I don't want to pretend to be something I'm not. Especially if it means I can't have you."

Carter didn't want to hope. He was afraid to let himself. "I can't keep being your secret, Josie."

"I'm not asking you to be. I came here this morning to invite you to church with me."

He blinked at her. Then he blinked some more. "What?"

Josie smiled, even though it did little to alleviate her general appearance of misery. "I talked to my mom. Really talked to her about things that I—let's just say that she helped me see myself a little more clearly. And she also told me that if I wanted to be with you, I needed to just do it and stop hiding. She also said that there isn't a more public way of announcing to the whole of Fontaine that you're seeing someone than going to church together."

Carter couldn't wrap his head around that. Not any of it. Not Deborah Marcum telling her daughter to date him openly. He sure as hell couldn't fathom Josie asking him to attend church with her. By Fontaine's standards, that was practically announcing an engagement.

"You're gonna have to run that by me again," he finally managed.

She rolled her eyes and then enunciated very carefully. "Will you go to church with me?"

"When?"

"Tomorrow is Sunday," she said.

Carter felt panic rearing. He hadn't stepped foot in a church other than attending funerals since he was a kid. But to walk into church with the preacher's daughter and sit there during the sermon under his disapproving eye? That just sounded like the very definition of hell.

"I'll make you a deal, Josie. I'll go to church with you tomorrow morning if you go out with me tonight. I'll pick you up, take you to dinner. We'll sit out in public in full view of everyone and act like two people who don't have a thing to hide."

The smile that curved her lips was so beautiful it took his breath away. She looked happy and freer than he'd ever seen her.

"I'd like that. I'd like that a lot. But now, I have to get to work. If I'm late, Doris will murder me."

"Probably not murder...Doris's real talent lies in just making you wish you were dead."

Josie walked over to him and stood up on her tiptoes. She kissed his cheek and then wrinkled her nose. "Carter, I hope you're planning on taking a shower sometime soon because you reek."

"I'll get on that," he said. "How much wine did you drink last night, Josie?"

"Enough that I'm going to have to use all my patience and a lot of prayer to survive Doris today," she quipped as she turned toward the door. "Where are you taking me tonight?"

"Dress up. Nice. It's not every day you get to take the person you're in love with on a first date," he called after her, ignoring the fact that raising his voice made his head feel like it was going to split wide open. Some things were just worth it.

Josie was still smiling. It had been hours since she'd confronted Carter at his apartment, since she'd found all the courage she needed to just say to hell with it. People would talk, and she would let them. If they were talking about her and Carter, it was because they didn't have enough going on in their own lives to keep them entertained. Not even Doris could dampen her mood.

At that thought, Josie looked up and caught Doris giving her the stink eye from the circulation desk. Okay, maybe Doris could dampen her mood. But really, that wasn't important in the overall scheme of things, because Doris could dampen anyone's mood. With her beady eyes, too stiff hair, turned down mouth, and the general air of discontent that hovered around her, Doris was a walking and talking depressant.

Taking another book from the cart, Josie re-shelved it where it belonged. It was an annoying aspect of her job that re-shelving books was all she was permitted to do. She had a degree in library science. She had ideas for programs to make the library better, to bring people there, and make it the center of their community. But as long as Doris reigned supreme, none of that would ever happen.

Picking up another book, Josie glanced at the cover. It was a torrid romance novel, the couple on the front locked in a heated embrace. That would be her. Tonight. It had been almost a week since she'd been in Carter's arms. And she needed him.

"For Pete's sake, Josephine! How long does it take you to re-shelve a book?"

Josie looked up to see Doris at the end of the stacks. The weight of disapproval in her stare was tangible. At any other time, Josie would have backed down immediately. She would have apologized and promised to do better. But the truth was, there was nothing wrong with the rate at which she was re-shelving books. There was nothing wrong with her job performance at all. She was actually more qualified to be head librarian than Doris, which was most certainly a big part of the problem she had with Josie.

"I'm sorry, Doris. Am I not scurrying quickly enough for you?" Josie asked, her voice saccharine sweet.

Sarcasm was apparently lost on Doris. "No, you're not. You're dawdling and taking your own sweet time about this, and there are more carts to be re-shelved!"

Josie looked pointedly at the circulation desk where Doris's sister-in-law and her cousin, both library employees, were poring over the donated magazines and divvying up the best ones between them.

"And there are more employees who can get to them... or do I need to approach the county commissioner about the fact that your relatives are part-time employees who act more like patrons?"

"I can't fire you," Doris said. "Not without their

approval, but I can make your life a living hell every moment that you're here."

"And that would be different, how? You'll give me dirty looks? You'll pawn all the crap jobs off on me while your family stuffs their faces and read the latest tabloids? Oh, I know. You'll remind me every day that I'm not wanted here, and you'll do whatever you can to get rid of me!" Josie was shouting by the time she reached the end of her list. "But you already *do* those things, Doris. Every day I come to work, I stand here, re-shelving books like a trained monkey while your idiot cousin, who's never read an actual book in her *life,* is in charge of acquisitions. You haven't offered any new community events that aren't a stale rehash of what you've done for the last seventeen years."

"Get your things and go home," Doris snapped. "I can't fire you, but I can suspend you. And if the commissioner doesn't like it, now I have witnesses to your unprofessional behavior. And don't think you fooled anyone here. We all know you've been carrying on with Carter Hayes!"

"You're right," Josie said. "I have been carrying on with him. In my house. His house. In his truck. Wherever and whenever we can! But I haven't done it here at the library, Doris, so you can't use that against me. What I do on my own time, in my personal life, has no bearing on my ability to do my job here. The only thing that keeps me from being an asset to this library is the fact that you're such a nepotistic jackass you won't let me be! And you go ahead and suspend me. With pay. I'll be filing a formal complaint with the county commissioner about the hostile work environment you've created here, and I'll be formally requesting an audit of just how library funds have been spent."

Josie marched past Doris. As an afterthought, she turned around and thrust the steamy romance novel at her. "You should read that. It might improve your disposition."

Gathering her purse and her coat from behind the desk, she ignored the curious stares and all the whispers from all the people who had somehow gathered in the library's central hall while she'd been all but shouting at her boss. One day, she thought, I will learn to control my temper and my mouth. But she was glad she hadn't done it yet. Doris needed to be told off, among other things.

As she walked out, Josie realized exactly what she'd done and all that she'd said. It would be all over town. She had to warn Carter, but first, she had to get to the county commissioner's office before Doris twisted everything around on her. Before she did anything, though, she was going home to change into something that didn't induce depression. If she never put on another pair of those god-awful khaki pants as long as she lived, she'd be a happy woman.

One of these days, she thought, I will learn to just keep my mouth shut.

Fifteen

Carter was moving another cabinet for Savannah. She'd decided that the antique quilts didn't need to be displayed on a rack but should be folded up in an armoire the way they might be displayed in someone's home. She'd also changed her mind about fifteen times on which piece of furniture she wanted to use for the display and where in the store she wanted it.

The bell above the door chimed again, and Carter looked up, noting the remarkable number of people milling about. All of them seemed to be giving him the side eye and whispering.

What the fuck was going on?

"What have you done?" Savannah asked.

Carter snapped his head back around and glared at her, ignoring the stabbing pain behind his eyes. "Why do you just assume I did something?"

Savannah leaned in and grabbed him by the ear the same way their grandmother used to. "The last time we had this much foot traffic on a non-holiday, it was right

130

after Bennett dove into the creek after Mia. People aren't here to buy furniture, Carter. They're here for gossip. So...what have you done? Oh, this better not be bad!"

He didn't know. Truly. But he had a sneaking suspicion that the truth about him and Josie had hit the fan. He swatted at Savannah's hands.

"Let go of my damn ear! Jesus! You're vicious!"

"Tell me, Carter," Savannah demanded. "I am not playing with you!"

"I really don't know," he said quietly. "But I suspect that maybe they might have heard I'm dating Josie Marcum."

Savannah glowered at him. "Everyone else's definition of dating, Carter, or yours?"

"What the hell does that mean?" he demanded.

"Most people call dating going out to dinner, being quasi-committed, and monogamous. You call it dating if you're willing to go back for the underwear you left behind rather than writing it off as a loss."

"I'm dating Josie," he said. "We've been seeing each other discreetly for a while, but I'm taking her on a real date tonight. And I'm going to church with her in the morning."

He watched as Savannah opened and then closed her mouth several times, not quite able to speak. Finally, she blinked at him and asked. "Church, really? With her dad staring down at you from the pulpit?"

Yeah, the thought of *that* made him sweat.

"I know. But this is serious, Van. She's it for me."

"How long has this been going on?" she asked in a whisper.

"About a month and a half."

Considering that he'd barely ever gone out with the same woman more than twice, and he had never referred to any woman as being *it* for him, they both knew what he was saying.

"Holy shit."

"I need to take off. I've got to get some things ready before tonight, and I don't think me being in here is such a good idea."

She looked at all the people just milling around, not buying anything. One of them was so busy watching Carter that she backed into a glass-fronted cabinet, sending everything in it wobbling.

"Go. Get the hell out before they wreck everything."

Carter went out the back, using the workroom exit to get to the alley and his truck. He stopped short at the sight of Josie standing there. It was just after lunch, which meant she was late going back, an unlikely occurrence, or she wasn't going back.

"You playing hooky from work, cupcake?"

She was wearing her coat open over the sweater dress that clung to every curve and a pair of black high-heeled boots that made him think very dirty things. Leaning against the hood of his truck, she looked like a pinup girl from days gone by. His eyes raked over her from head to toe, and it dawned on him that he didn't want to date Josie. He wanted to marry her.

"I kind of think I might not be employed anymore," she admitted. "I, in perfectly professional terminology, kind of told Doris to kiss my ass."

"You're feeling a little impulsive today, aren't you?" he asked. There was an idea flitting around in his mind. It was crazy. It was completely crazy. But then, so were they. Everything about them defied convention.

"Just a little bit. I may also have managed to get her fired. At the very least, I'm getting her ass audited."

That raised his eyebrows. "Remind me not to piss you

off. On the off chance, did your telling her to kiss your ass also involve you telling her about me? Because half of Fontaine is traipsing through the store right now, trying to get the scoop."

Josie closed her eyes, leaned her head back against the truck, and let out a frustrated groan. "What is wrong with people, Carter? Why is everyone so tangled up in everybody else's business?"

"Come upstairs with me," he said.

"You're not getting out of taking me on an actual date. Even if you do con me into your bed, we're still going somewhere for dinner," she insisted.

"I'd never dream of starving you, baby. But hanging out in an alley is hardly going to improve either one of our reputations."

She shrugged to concede the point and then preceded him up the stairs. Inside, he took her coat and draped it over the rack behind the door. "Sit your butt on that couch and just close your eyes for a minute. I have something for you."

"Are you trying to trick me into giving you a blow job?" she asked.

He laughed. "That hadn't been my plan, but now that you bring it up, it sounds like a great idea."

When Josie was on the couch, eyes closed, Carter retreated to the bedroom and dug through the dresser drawers until he found what he wanted. The engagement ring had belonged to his father's mother. It was the only thing he had from his father, but more to the point, it was the only engagement ring he could lay hands on at the moment.

Walking back into the living room, she was still sitting there, eyes closed, and a vaguely amused smile on her face.

"What's so funny?"

"I was just thinking that I don't know whether you're a bad good influence or a good bad influence on me...but whatever you are, I like it."

Carter dropped down onto one knee in front of her. "I'm kind of glad you said that, all things considered. Open your eyes, Josie."

She did. He saw confusion first as she looked at him kneeling in front of her, and then the tiniest spark of hope flared in her eyes.

"Carter, what are you doing?"

"When I saw you down there, waiting for me as I left work, I thought, I don't want to date this girl. I want to marry her. So I'm asking, Josephine Marcum, if instead of going out to dinner with me tonight, if you'll get in my truck with me, and drive to Tennessee...and come back as my wife."

She stared at him for a minute before speaking. "On one condition."

"What's that?" he asked, fearing the worst.

"We can't take your truck all the way to Tennessee, Carter. We'll never make it there."

Carter didn't argue the point. He would lose. Instead, he took the ring from the small box as Josie held out her left hand. He slipped it on her finger, and it fit perfectly, like it had been meant for her.

"It's not much—"

"It's everything," she corrected. "Let's just go. Right now. I don't want to wait another minute. I love you, and I know it's quick, and I know people will say we're crazy, but I don't care. I just want to be with you."

He kissed her, claiming her lips, hungry for the taste of her. But she pulled back.

"Don't sidetrack me, Carter Hayes. We're not doing any more of that until this ring is legal and binding."

Carter rose to his feet and pulled her up with him. "Did I mention that I'm really looking forward to being bossed around by you for the next fifty years or so?"

"Nope. But I'll remind you of that whenever it's necessary," she retorted.

They left his apartment, took the steps down to the alley, and climbed into her car. She let him drive since she couldn't pull her eyes away from the ring that winked on her left hand.

"Are we really gonna do this?" she asked.

"I can't think of anything I want to do more," he answered honestly.

"Then drive. Get me the hell out of this town and make an honest woman of me."

She didn't have to ask him twice.

It had taken them close to two hours to get to Tennessee. They'd crossed the border into a tiny little town that wasn't even half the size of Fontaine. But when they'd stopped at the rest area and talked to the security guard, he'd told them where to go.

They'd gotten to the county clerk's office with five minutes to spare and gotten the license. Now, standing in the middle of a grocery store, between a sale display of snack cakes and leftover fireworks, the grocery store manager, who was also an ordained minister, was looking at them like they were crazy.

"We can go to the church. It's just down the street."

Carter looked at Josie, and she shook her head. "She wants to do this here...and I try to give her what she wants. It goes better for me that way."

The manager-slash-minister scratched his head for a second, as if he were completely confounded by them. "All right. I'll do my best to remember all the words."

Carter took Josie's hand in his. He had the matching band to her engagement ring in his pocket. She didn't have one for him, but they'd remedy that later.

"Dearly beloved—" He stopped because there was no one gathered. Over the electronic hum of all the coolers and the beeping of cash registers in the distance, they could hear the wonky wheel of a grocery cart rolling past in another aisle. "Just join hands."

Josie looked pointedly at their hands that were already linked. The minister blushed, and Carter did his best not to grin like an idiot.

The minister looked at the license. "Do you, Carter, take this woman, Josephine Odette Marcum, to be your lawfully wedded wife, forsaking all others, to have and to hold, for richer, for poorer, in sickness and in health, so long as you both shall live?"

"I do," Carter said with complete certainty.

The minister nodded, clearly satisfied with that answer. "Do you, Josephine, take this man, Carter Jefferson Hayes, to be your lawfully wedded husband, forsaking all others, to have and to hold, for richer, for poorer, in sickness and in health, so long as you both shall live?"

"I do," Josie said.

"Do you have a ring, son? 'Cause we don't sell those here," the man offered, more than a little concerned. He clearly thought they were insane, and he wasn't entirely wrong.

Carter couldn't keep from laughing at that. "I've got that covered," he said and pulled the matching band from his pocket.

The minister nodded, clearly relieved that at least some part of the whole thing seemed to be going according to plan.

"Place the ring—"

A tinny voice came over the loudspeaker. "Clean up on aisle five, please. Clean up on aisle five."

The intercom shut off, and the minister just shook his head. "Why you'd want to do this here, I'll never know."

"It makes about as much sense as we do," Josie answered. "Trust me, this is it."

"Place the ring on the third finger of her left hand." Carter did so. "I now pronounce you husband and wife. You may kiss your bride."

Carter didn't hesitate. He swung Josie up into his arms and kissed her like his life depended on it. "I love you, Josie Marcum."

"Hayes," she corrected. "Josie Marcum-Hayes."

He grinned. "Your parents are going to kill us."

She nodded. "Probably. So make my wedding night count."

Carter reached behind her and grabbed a package of cupcakes from the display rack.

"It's not exactly a wedding cake, but it'll do for now."

She laughed. "It'll do. It'll definitely do. Where do we go now? Home?"

"Whose home?" he asked with a frown. "Where are we gonna live?"

She smiled. "I really like your apartment...but I need closets."

"I'll build you one," he offered.

"Then take me home."

Eating cupcakes in the car, the drive back to Fontaine seemed infinitely longer. Maybe it was because Carter knew exactly what was waiting for him on their return.

Josie sang along with the radio, her voice sweet and soulful. He hadn't known she could sing. There were many things he didn't know about her, but that didn't cause alarm or make him question what they'd just done. Instead, he was looking forward to discovering new things about her every day.

Josie started to laugh. She kept laughing until tears were streaming down her face.

"What the hell is so funny?"

She was gasping for breath, trying to form words.

"Clean up...clean up on aisle five."

Sixteen

Carter parked Josie's car behind his truck and climbed out of the vehicle. Walking around to the passenger side, he opened the door for her. Once she stepped out, he scooped her up into his arms.

"You're only supposed to carry me over the threshold, not down the alley, up the flight of stairs, etcetera, etcetera," she reproved.

"I like carrying you," he said. "It reminds me of the first night I ever brought you home with me. Of course, I'm going to hope that this night goes a little differently."

She laughed. "You don't think puking and passing out are appropriate wedding night activities?"

He paused at the top of the stairs. "My keys are in my pocket."

Before Josie could ask what he meant, he shifted her in his arms, and suddenly she was draped over his shoulder in a fireman's carry. One strong arm gripped her at the backs of her thighs, and she was staring directly at his denim-clad behind.

"Carter Hayes, this is not romantic."

"Of course it is," he said as he unlocked the door. "We're nonconformists."

"I'm dizzy. All the blood is rushing to my head!"

His hand moved from the backs of her thighs up to her bottom, cupping one cheek. "Funny, I'm having the same problem."

Once inside the apartment, he dropped the keys on the table and then lowered her until she could put her feet on the floor. Standing upright, Josie really was dizzy. She placed one hand on his shoulder and leaned back against the door.

"I am not a sack of potatoes or a bale of hay," she informed him. "You don't just prop me on your shoulder and carry me around like that!"

Carter was still kneeling in front of her, but he was clearly distracted. His hands were on her thighs, skimming beneath her dress.

Good lord, she thought, his hands. Callused and rough, but always gentle when it counted. As he pushed the hem of her dress up, he hooked his thumbs through the sides of her panties and slowly tugged them down over her hips. They snagged on her boots, and she reached for the zipper to take them off, but Carter stopped her.

"Oh, you're leaving the boots on," he said. "They've been driving me crazy since I saw you leaning against my truck."

She wanted to say something funny, something witty and smart, but he was kissing her thighs. His mouth was hot on her skin. The soft glide of his tongue on her inner thighs was maddening. She pressed her palms against the door and closed her eyes, letting the sensation wash over her.

Each pass of his tongue, of his lips, and the gentle nip of his teeth moved higher, closer to the part of her that was so eager for him. He hooked one hand behind her knee and draped one of her legs over his shoulder, opening her to him. Then his mouth was on her. If he'd been gentle and tender while kissing her thighs, he was now ravenous. His mouth moved over her hungrily, his tongue circling her clit, sucking deeply as if he wanted to consume her.

Josie buried her fingers in his hair, holding onto him as the world just fell away. She couldn't think. Couldn't speak. She just trembled against him as he devoured her. The intensity of her orgasm was shocking. Her body quaked. Had it not been for his hand pressed against her stomach, holding her up, she would have collapsed right there. What was even more shocking was that he was not stopping. He continued the sensual onslaught, drawing out the pleasure until it was almost too much to bear.

Sobbing, breathless, unable to form coherent words, she just begged. "No more. Carter...it's too much."

Her reprieve was only momentary. Carter picked her up, carried her to the couch and lay down with her, his hard body pressed against hers. Her dress just vanished. Her bra followed. Lying there beneath him, wearing nothing but a pair of high-heeled boots, she felt decadent, sexy, and all those things that she'd always wanted to feel.

As she looked up at him, their eyes met, and it wasn't just the hunger that she saw there. It was so much more.

"I never dreamed that when I pulled you down off that bar, this is where we'd end up. But I wouldn't change a damn second of it. You're perfect, Josie. And you're mine."

"God, I love you," she whispered. "Even when you make me crazy...maybe especially when you make me crazy."

There was no more talking. Carter stripped off his

shirt, revealing the hard, lean muscles that just robbed her of the ability to think. His jeans followed, and then he was naked against her, skin to skin.

Locking her legs around his lean hips, she pulled him close. He surged into her, deep, hard, and it was so perfect. She held onto him as he rocked into her again and again, each thrust reawakening the intense pleasure of only moments earlier.

He kissed her neck, her collarbone, the curve of her jaw. And then his mouth was on hers, tasting her, teasing. His tongue moved between her parted lips, mimicking the actions of his body. It drove her over the edge, and she was shuddering beneath him, moaning his name against his lips.

She felt him stiffen against her, his muscles going completely rigid, and then the hot rush of his release inside her.

Afterward, curled together on the couch, Carter traced lazy circles on her hips, tickling her spine and generally being an adorable nuisance.

"We still have to tell everybody we got married."

"We could," he said. "Or we could just let Fontaine's gossip mill do the work for us. If they're going to talk about us, Josie, we ought to at least benefit from it."

It was such a tempting idea. "Isn't that a little cowardly?"

"Hell, yes, it is...and I am okay with that."

She turned over so that they were facing one another, resting her arms on his chest as his hand shifted to her hair, twining the strands around his fingers.

"So...who do we tell to get the word out?"

Carter reached for his pants lying on the floor and fished his cell phone from his pocket. He scrolled through his contacts and then tapped Bennett's name.

The phone rang twice before Bennett answered. "This better be good."

Knowing what he'd more than likely interrupted, Carter grinned. "You've been walking around with blue balls for years. A few more minutes won't kill you. I need to speak to Mia."

"No," Bennett said. "Call back later."

Carter laughed, but pressed on. "Seriously, Bennett. This is important."

Bennett sighed. "Fine. But you owe me."

A second later, Mia picked up the phone. "Is something wrong?"

"No. Nothing is wrong, but we need you to spread a little gossip for us."

"Who is *we*?" she asked.

"Do you think you could tell people who would then tell other people that Josie and I eloped today?"

Mia's squeal was deafening. "You didn't!"

"We did, actually. And since everyone in town wants to talk about us anyway, we figured we'd kill two birds with one stone."

"I'll call Loralei...and Annalee. But you do know that shit is going to hit the fan over this, right? I mean, her dad is a minister, and you went and got married in a courthouse!"

"A grocery store, actually," Carter corrected. "It's a long story."

After a few more pertinent details were exchanged, the call ended, and Carter looked at Josie. "It's done. By tomorrow morning, the entire town will know."

She rolled her eyes. "By ten o'clock tonight, the whole town will know!"

"It's eight thirty now, so yeah, probably. I'm ordering pizza. I did promise not to let you starve," he said.

Josie sat up and unzipped the boots that had gone from decadent and sexy to just hot and uncomfortable.

"At least when we go to church tomorrow, there'll be witnesses, and my daddy can't shoot you on the spot."

His face fell. "We still have to go to church?"

"*Yes*. And I'm not going to face this alone," she said, as she got up from the couch. "I need a shower. Then you're going to feed me, and then we're going to bed where we may or may not sleep. I haven't decided yet."

Carter watched her walking naked across the living room. "Yes, ma'am."

If getting that view meant he had to go and be preached to, he'd just learn to live with it.

Epilogue

J osie straightened Carter's tie for the third time. As he reached up to tug at it, she smacked his hand. "Leave it alone! It looks fine."

"It feels like a damn noose."

She glanced pointedly at the church they were parked beside. "You want to rephrase that?"

"No. I don't. I can still cuss till we're inside," he said.

They'd arrived early. Josie figured facing her father down before the sermon would be their best option. As they walked toward the front steps, the side door of the church opened, and she saw her mother standing there. Deborah waved them over.

Carter gripped her hand tightly.

"I'm okay," she said.

"Well, I'm not," he shot back, and his voice was tight with nerves.

"They won't bite," she offered reassuringly.

"Will they shoot?" he demanded.

"Not in church. Come on," she said. "Dreading it is always worse than just doing it."

He looked ahead to where her mother stood waiting for them. "I think you might be wrong about that."

As they reached the building, Deborah stepped back to let them inside. The door had no sooner closed behind them than she was grabbing Josie's left hand and looking at the ring that rested on her third finger.

"It's true. I thought it was just a rumor, but...why would you run off like that?" she asked, clearly hurt.

"It wasn't like that," Josie said. "We just wanted to be married. No fuss, no fanfare, and delays."

"But I always pictured your wedding—"

"I didn't want a wedding, Mom," Josie said, hugging her mother. "I just wanted to be married to Carter."

Deborah hugged her back and then sniffed. "You're still having a wedding. It might be after the fact, but maybe for your first anniversary, we can have a real wedding...in this church," she said pointedly and looked directly at Carter.

He wisely didn't respond with anything more than a nod of agreement.

"Your daddy is waiting upstairs," Deborah said.

"Are his feelings hurt?" Josie asked.

"Oddly enough, no. He took it much better than I did. But men don't understand what weddings mean." She glanced at Carter. "No offense."

"None taken. I don't understand weddings. At all."

When they entered the church hall with her mother, the buzz of conversation stopped. A pin drop would have sounded like a bomb, it went so quiet.

"Yeah, not awkward at all," Carter whispered.

Josie jabbed her elbow into his side. "Behave."

"You married the wrong man for that," he answered.

Beside them, Deborah smiled. She'd had her doubts, but hearing that exchange told her everything she needed to know. They were easy with one another, comfortable in a way that could only happen if they were meant to be for one another.

William walked forward, hugged Josie tightly, and then shook Carter's hand. Behind them, the congregation began to talk again, the roar of it deafening.

"We've definitely given them all something to talk about," Josie said softly.

Carter grinned. "It won't be the last time. That I can promise you."

Author's Note

The little town at the end of this book, where Carter and Josie elope, is based on an actual place...my hometown. It never failed that wherever I have gone in this world, someone I have met has either gotten married there or knew someone who had. We did, honestly, have a justice of the peace who performed marriage ceremonies in the grocery store on Main Street. Both the grocery store and the justice of the peace are gone, but I wanted to incorporate those elements of my hometown and its history into this book because Carter and Josie just seemed to fit that mold.

Also, in regard to Josie's adoption, that plot point was one I debated putting in there. But after communicating with people who have adopted children internationally and hearing so many tales that are just like Josie's, of it being perceived as a completely charitable act as opposed to just another way to add to your family, I felt that I made the right choice. Additionally, since writing this book, my husband and I have adopted a child of our own. Our son is a blessing to us every day, and I feel that God put us in a place to receive that blessing. I think we were meant to find our way to one another, and I hope that other families feel the same.

If it isn't reflective of your experience, then I'm incredibly happy for you. If it is reflective of your experience, then I apologize for all the people in this world who simply don't understand that family is so much more than just blood.

A Look at Book Four

QUENTIN

She's the only one who makes him feel. He's the last man she should trust.

Quentin Darcy hides his demons behind a perfect smile. Charm, good looks, and a reputation as the smoothest operator around —he wears them like armor. But one tough-talking bartender has always seen right through him. Harlowe Tate. Straight shooter. Big heart. Bad at staying out of trouble. And trouble's exactly what finds her when her ex comes back looking for blood.

Quentin knows commitment isn't in his DNA. He's built walls no one's ever broken through. But Lowey? She's never been just anyone. And now, protecting her might cost him everything he's tried so hard to bury. Because in their world, loyalty cuts deep, revenge runs darker, and some battles can't be won without shedding a little blood.

She's risking her life. He's risking his soul. And neither of them is ready for the fallout.

AVAILABLE OCTOBER 2025

Chasity Bowlin is a *USA Today* bestselling author of numerous romance novels. She resides in central Kentucky with her husband, their charming son, and a lively menagerie of animals. A passionate traveler, Chasity enjoys weaving glimpses of her real-life adventures into her stories. As an avid Anglophile, she adores all things British, with a particular love for the Regency era.

Born and raised in Tennessee, Chasity spent much of her childhood with her doting grandparents, where soap operas and back-to-back episodes of Scooby-Doo were part of her daily routine. Her path to becoming a romance novelist was perhaps inevitable—her Barbie dolls didn't just cruise in pink convertibles; they traveled through time, hosted extravagant dinner parties, and one even had an evil twin locked in the attic.

www.chasitybowlin.com

www.ingramcontent.com/pod-product-compliance
Lightning Source LLC
Chambersburg PA
CBHW010828250626
47169CB00010B/2993